Faces

of

Shame

A Novel By

TONYA PHILLIPS

 **OPAL BOOK PUBLISHING**

Copyright © 2012 by Tonya Phillips

Editor: Corinthia A. Kelley

ISBN 10: 0-9727011-5-X
ISBN 13: 978-0-9727011-5-0

Printed in the United States

Opal Book Publishing
Temple Hills, Maryland
www.obpublishing.com

Acknowledgements

I would like to start off with praising and thanking my God, the creator, because without Him, none of this would have been possible!

Brian, Tylanya, and Terrance...mommy loves you so much! *Anthony Young*, Thank you so much for being the love of my life. You are truly a wonderful, loving, and caring man who definitely treats me like the Queen that I am. You've been very supportive and I couldn't ask for anything more. To my Mom and Dad (*Vivian & Roosevelt*), my sisters (*Shanetta* and *Neesha*), and my brother (*Gerry*), Your sister is doing it! Thank you so much for your continued love and your support of what I do. My best friend *Melissa Howard*, You have been there with me through thick and thin for thirty years of our friendship. You are my sister, a genuine star, elegant, classy, and most of all...a Beautiful person and I thank you so much for your support! *Tanora Gibbs*, Thank you so much for introducing me to *Author Corinthia A. Kelley*, and for being such a good friend for many of years. You know we go way back girl. You are truly a beautiful person! *Melissa Prophet*, Thank you for being my friend and for being there to listen. You are witty, smart, intelligent, as well as a good person. *Theresa Smothers*, Thank you so much for your added support and the good meals that you love to cook. I'm looking forward to becoming part of the family real soon! *Chandra Wilson*, Thank you also for all of your support while working on this project and for giving me that extra push. *Antonio Lyons,* (b.k.a. Romeo), Thank you so much for keeping my hair done, whenever I needed it to be. You are truly wonderful! *Angela McNeill* and *August Pitts*, Thank you for your support as well. Last, but not least, I would like to thank my publishing company, *Opal Book Publishing*, for signing me with the company and believing in my project!

Faces

of

Shame

CHAPTERS

Overtime   1

Sherita's Problems   9

The Perfect Couple   19

Mama Dorothy's Release   27

Monica's Trip   33

Club Night w/Sherita   41

Drop In The Bucket   51

More Drama   57

What Happened in Las Vegas?   67

A Night Out   73

Pointing Fingers   101

The Big Move   115

Surprise Visit   121

A New Day   141

Mommy   153

Together Again   161

CHAPTER ONE

~Overtime~

The phone rung, after letting it ring at least ten times before rolling over to answer it. It was my supervisor wanting me to put in extra hours at the post office.

"Shit!" I said to myself.

I was hoping that it may have been a date, but unfortunately it wasn't. Out of all of the men that I've met, half of them just want a booty call anyway and I wasn't having it. No matter what, I will never be like my so-called mother. Mama Dorothy is what we called her. All she wanted to do is get high on cocaine, heroin, and drink her vodka, gin, and beer. I was so glad that she was in rehab because if she wasn't, I would've had to watch every damn thing I owned in my apartment, down to my underwear. I made a promise that I would raise my children, Michelle and Javon, who were six and three years of age, much better than she raised the three of us. I vowed that I would never take my children through all of the turmoil that Mama Dorothy took us through. Although when she had Mike, she was married to his father. I guess that's why he turned out to be so successful. When Sherita and I came along, we didn't even know who our fathers were and neither did my mother. Sherita couldn't stand her

1

guts, but I still loved my mother, even 'til this day. My mother never dated, or whored with anybody in her own age range. They were always younger than she was.

As I got into my Tahoe truck, which needed to be washed, my best friend Lavern pulled up in her Mazda 626, which was all black and decked out. I've known Lavern since the ninth grade. We were both single by the way. I guess we just haven't found that true love yet. She has twin boys and was always ready to go somewhere. She was just like my sister Sherita, on the go. I'm more of a laid back type of person. I would rather have a husband to lie under and cuddle with every night.

Sherita has a friend named Cecil. I feel like he's just a waste of her time, tearing down her self-esteem, always asking for money, and smokes more weed than Mexico can grow it. I don't see how she does it, but she just accepts it anyway. I could see if he had something going on with himself, like our brother Mike. He landed himself a wife, even though Karen is a bit snobbish and self-centered. She's alright with me, but not with Sherita.

Karen is bit upscale. She's a beautiful, long haired, light-skinned woman with full lips and has a booming body right out of a jet magazine. Those were the attributes that my brother loved about her. Mike is tall, brown-skinned, and very muscular. I'm not so tall. I'm about five feet, six inches tall, brown skinned, cute in the face and so is Sherita. A lot of people thought we were twins sometimes, but we're actually a year apart. Mama Dorothy is only about five feet four inches tall and was much heavier back in her day. Now she's small and I had no idea at the time that smoking crack made people lose that much weight. I hope she gained some weight since being in rehab, which she's due to come out within the next six months. Sherita won't be too happy about that and neither will Karen. She looked up to Mama Dorothy at one time. However, when those drugs took over, everyone turned on her, which I couldn't blame them for doing. Cecil on the other hand didn't care, because when he was on the streets at one point, he sold her the crack. Hell, he ain't amounting to much anyway, but in Sherita's eyes, he's her everything. So was her son Delonte, who she never spanked or disciplined. She would let him get away with almost everything.

I can remember one time when he and Javon spilled milk on Mike and Karen's Broyhill Italian leather sofa. I spanked Javon and all she did was stare at me. She was so busy chasing Cecil's 'no good' ass around, that she had no time for anything or anybody else. Karen was so upset that you could see the lines forming in her forehead. I wanted to laugh, but the mere fact of the boys spilling milk wasn't even funny. It was Karen's facial expression that was hysterical.

Later on that night, Lavern and I decided to go to dinner and then out to a place on Carver Ave.

"Come on girl. This will be fun," she said. "Plus I wanna see if this fine ass Jamaican guy is going to be there tonight".

He wore dreads and had one nice ass bottom piece.

3

"Damn Lavern, you act like you seen it or been with him before or something…"

"Naw! Monica it ain't like that, but you could tell he's very well in endowed though," Lavern laughed.

"Looks don't mean much," I said. "You're always looking for love. Let love find you for once. Better yet, stop being so damn horny because chances are that these men are just as horny as you are, and that's it, so face it."

"Monica, grow up! You keep thinking you will find a husband and it's not that easy," Lavern responded with a slight attitude and a bit of arrogance.

"Karen found my brother and that's because they are equal. They're financially perfect, both are health nuts, and sincere to one another. A lot of men are looking for women that have as much stability as they have."

"Okay, see…" Lavern pointed in the air, "I just want to date. When you date, you can't go wrong."

"Oh please Lavern…you are looking for a man just as well as I am".

"No, not really! When you're dating, there's no confusion on where you've been, what time you're coming home, don't wear that, you can't go, all of that. I grew tired of that same ole shit Monica. That's a man that wants to control a woman. When I was with Kenny and Kyle's

4

father," she said, "I got knocked down sometimes with one punch. Shit, I just want some dick now and then."

"I don't know Lavern, I want somebody who holds me, touches me, who loves me, a secured man, and a God-fearing man with all the goodness. When Aaron left me for another woman, I thought my life was over. He left me to care for our kids. I love Michelle and Javon, but I still need somebody."

"Does he help take care of them?" Lavern asked.

"Yeah he does. He picks them up every other weekend. I just hate when his wife is in the car. I didn't know my father and neither does Mama Dorothy."

"Girl, I'm sorry about your mother," Lavern said showing concern.

"Shit, she's been like that before I was born. I'm now twenty five and my mother is still on drugs."

"Damn I hope she gets herself together," Lavern said.

"Sometimes I wish she were more like your mother. Your mother has a real-estate business and she's been married to the same man for twenty years".

I couldn't do anything but fall into Lavern's arms and cry at this point, which was the case most of time. I stayed depressed because of Mama Dorothy. I can't turn my back on her like my sister did.

"How long are you talking about hanging out tonight?"

"Until about four, Lavern replied. "Girl, it's only seven now. It's still early."

"Oh no...I have to work overtime tomorrow as well as the weekend. Speaking of Aaron, he's picking the kids up at ten tonight. So we can go somewhere and eat dinner."

"Damn Monica, I hate when you have to work every other weekend and overtime at that. Does Aaron pick them every other weekend?"

"Only on the weekends that I have to work. I only get Monday's off whenever I work the whole weekend. Maybe the weekend that I don't have to work, we can hang out. Call Stephanie with her hot ass. I'm sure she'll love to hang out tonight with you.

Stephanie was one of our school buddies. Now she's living well with no children and still looking for somebody just like we were. She's also a go getter. Whatever she wants, she gets! She drives a candy apple Porsche. She didn't make much money, but both Lavern and I knew the guy she was dating. At one time, he was a dope dealer. He helped her to buy that car and not only that, he laid out her crib as well. I doubt if she ever wants children though.

Lavern and I pulled up in front of Red Lobster. I parked my truck right beside her shiny black Mazda 626. Seeing my car next to hers looked awkward, especially since mine needed a good wash and wax done to it. I won't be able to get it done until Monday, when I'm off.

When Lavern and I left the restaurant, she went to see what was up with Stephanie so that they could hook up and go to the club. I so badly needed to get some rest until Aaron came to pick up the kids. I surely needed this Friday off. But at least I spent some time with Lavern.

When I got in the house and turned on the television, the first thing I saw was the depressing ass news. Then I wanted to take a nap, but I wasn't that tired. I looked out the window and saw how dirty my truck really was. I got my ass up and went to the car wash after I picked the kids up from the neighbor's house. When I got back in the house, there was a message beeping on my answering machine. It was Aaron explaining that he wasn't able to get the kids until Saturday night. He and his wife Brenda were going to some damn Convention at the last minute. She was Caucasian. It didn't bother me at first, but why the hell would he wait until today to let me know? Now I was pissed off after thinking about it for a minute. I guess I'd just have to call Aunt Vera to see if she would watch them. At least there was still a strong minded person in the family.

Aunt Vera was a retired RN. She was married to my Uncle Harold, until she lost him to her best friend Connie, and then he later died from prostate cancer. There were some in the family who said that Mama Dorothy also slept with Uncle Harold before he cheated with Connie, however, I don't know how true that was. That's one reason why Mama Dorothy and Aunt Vera got into an argument and no longer spoke. She had also stole four hundred dollars from Aunt Vera's purse once, to feed her drug habit. Sherita loves the ground Aunt Vera walks on. She practically raised us. She has one son and a daughter as well. They too, turned out to be successful people. They both now live in Southern California. When I called Aunt Vera, she agreed to watch the kids for me when I left for work. As far as Aaron was concerned, he was going to get a piece of my mind.

CHAPTER TWO

~Sherita's Problems~

I met Cecil back in 1998. He seemed to be a really nice man and treated me with respect all the time. Standing six foot two, tall and dark just the way I like them, he should have been a basketball player. Cecil was from the Bronx and his mother had higher standards and hope for both Cecil and his brother, until they both started selling drugs on the street at the young age of fourteen and fifteen. Not being able to deal with the situation any longer of her boys selling drugs for about a year, his mother sent him and his brother to live with their uncle in Ohio. That didn't turn out be a good idea because his uncle was just like that bitch of a mother that I had. Cecil's uncle started using drugs and overdosed within a year. Neither one of them finished school. Jason, Cecil's brother, got locked up for drug possession and murder, and was now serving time at Rikers Island. He was nicknamed in the streets and in prison as KYD, which stood for 'Kill You Dead'. He was just that ruthless!

"It's time to get up Cecil," Sherita yelled.

"Come on, leave me the hell alone," he said.

"Don't you have to go to work?"

"Yeah, I am in a minute."

Constantly nagging him, "No…Cecil, get up now. I'm tired of telling you to get up and go to work. You're a grown ass man!"

"You let Delonte sleep!"

"It's Saturday… why should I wake up my son?"

Cecil rolled over to face Sherita, "I don't care if it was the weekday, you'd still let his ass sleep."

"Don't be talking about my son," she grew a little irritated.

"See, that's your damn problem! You spoil his ass too much and that ain't good."

"That's my son, so don't be saying anything about my child."

"Ain't I his father? I mean I might as well be."

"But, you're not. His father ain't shit."

"I'm a good role model and father figure to him," Cecil sat up in the bed as his voice rose to make his point.

"Sometimes I wonder what you mean by that Cecil. I love you, but you have to get it together."

"And who said that shit, your family? Man, fuck your family," he decided to then climb out of the bed to get ready for work. Then he thought about it for a minute, "Speaking of your family, are you going to Mike and Karen's cookout?"

"No, I'll call Monica to see if she's going," Sherita turned towards the mirror.

"Why you don't want to go?"

"Stop asking me shit like that," she snapped.

"Girl...stop fuckin yelling! I told you about talking to me like I'm some child. What's wrong with you?"

"Nothing. Nothing at all Cecil."

Cecil stood at the closet in their room to pick out a shirt to wear.

"Oh, I know what's wrong! You feel bad because we over here living in a one bedroom apartment, while your sister over their living in a three-bedroom condo, driving her big ass Tahoe truck with no man. And last but not least, your brother and his wife, the stuck up ass fuckin' beauty queen, with their mini-mansion and shit. She got her jaguar and he got his Lexus SL truck. So what? We have each other. Things will get better for us baby, you'll see. We don't even have a car, but we'll get one," trying to make her feel a little better about herself.

"When Cecil? I really would like to know when the hell is it going to happen? When?"

Cecil sucked his teeth, "girl you crazy" he said as he walked into the bathroom to brush his teeth.

"No, you're crazy, and stop dropping all that toothpaste on the floor. Don't you know how to brush your teeth?"

Cecil didn't pay any attention to her comment and switched the subject.

"When is your mother getting out of rehab?"

"Why you wanna know? You helped feed her that poison?

"She did that shit to herself Sherita and you know it."

"Look, don't mention that bitch's name to me, okay?

"I asked the wrong thing huh?" he questioned.

"You sure did," she replied back.

"Well, I didn't feel like going to work today, but since I'm up, I better go. You lucky you don't work on weekends," he said before leaving out the front door.

When Cecil left, I couldn't wait to get my thoughts together. I'm getting tired of living like this. I suddenly called my sister to ask her about the big gathering over at Mike and Karen's.

"Hey sis…"

"Hey girl, are you going over to Mike and whatever her name is house?"

"It's next weekend, right?"

"Yeah, I have their precious little invitation right here," Sherita said sarcastically.

"Where's Cecil?"

"He just left for work, where he should be going."

"You should stop acting like that for real," Monica said as she let out a laugh. "Why are you so bitter with your own brother and his wife?"

"Because," she paused, "Karen puts her nose up at people because they don't have what she has.

"I don't have as much as them either Sherita."

"But Monica, you have a vehicle and a three bedroom condo. You're doing okay for yourself, especially not to have a man. I have one and still have to struggle day to day with our small ass incomes."

"You know what Sherita, you can stop this little charade of yours. Only you are the cause of your own happiness."

"But, I love Cecil. When we're having sex, it's so good. We have to go into the living room though when we do it because of the space, and we don't want to wake up Delonte. Our sex is awesome, but he needs to do better."

As she decided to change the subject, "What are you doing tomorrow?" Sherita asked Monica.

"I'm working overtime for the weekend".

"Is Aaron picking up the kids?"

"No, he's going to some damn convention with Brenda tonight."

"Don't you hate that shit?"

"What, that he's with another woman? I don't care anymore. I used to be bothered behind it, but not anymore. I called Aunt Vera and she said she would watch them for me."

"Speaking of Auntie, I need to call her and ask her to bake some cakes just in case I decide to go over to the *lifestyles of the rich and famous* house."

"Stop it, Sherita! You know mama will be home in about six months?"

"Who? That bitch's name is Dorothy to me, not mama."

Changing the subject on Monica once again, "Have you talked with Lavern lately?"

"I hung out with her for a little bit today. She's supposed to be going out to the club tonight, her and Stephanie."

"Oh shit, I should go out with them and see if Champagne wants to go too. Do you think you could call and ask if Aunt Vera can babysit Delonte for me? Please?," she begged Monica.

My friend Champagne lived with her mother and has five kids by five different men, no man, a part time job at the grocery store, still gets welfare from the County, and loves to go to the clubs. She and Monica are the same age and I don't see how she does it. Raising five kids? No help from either of the fathers? Her mother just lies around gaining weight. She's already carrying a hefty four hundred and fifty pounds. Champagne and her mother are both huge women, with Champagne weighing close to around three hundred pounds herself. She loves to party though.

As I attempted to pick up the phone to call Champagne, the operator on the other end was talking and saying *'you have a collect call from Ohio Prison facility from Cecil. Will you accept?'* I didn't even hear the phone ring before picking it up. My heart dropped and so did the telephone. I bent down to pick up the phone and accepted the call.

"What the hell are you doing in jail Cecil?"

"They trying to say that I stole four thousand and two hundred dollars from the cash register," he replied.

"Well...?" Sherita interrupted herself with her question, "I know how you like to smoke weed."

"What the…come on Sherita, this is my job we talking about. Come on yo! This shit is crucial."

"Cecil, if you stole that money, you're in big trouble. McDonald's is a world-wide restaurant chain…" Cecil interrupted her statement.

"Man ain't nobody tryin' to hear that shit. Just bring two hundred dollars up here so I can get out of here girl."

"I don't have any money Cecil. I just paid the rent remember? You couldn't help me because you said your check was short last pay day."

"You would have had it if you didn't go buy Delonte all those summer clothes."

"He needed that stuff."

"You spent four hundred and twenty two dollars on that shit. I know because the receipt is in the dresser drawer."

"So what Cecil, stop telling me what to spend on my son."

"Stop yelling Sherita, I told you about that and I'm not going to tell you again, you crazy bitch!"

"You have a nerve calling me and asking me for money and you locked up behind bars and still talking shit! Correct yourself on this man."

"Girl, just get the money."

"So you fired now huh?"

"I guess so Sherita," he said

"*How did I get myself in this situation*" was what I whispered to myself.

"Don't be mumbling girl, I can still hear yo ass."

"I'll call sis and see if she can loan it to me. Call me back in about thirty minutes Cecil."

Cecil agreed to give her a call back within the time frame that she specified. After hanging up the phone, Sherita rehearsed how she was going to even form her lips to ask Monica for the money to help Cecil out. She knew how her sister felt about Cecil and part of her felt that he was going to be stuck for a minute if she had to get the money from Monica.

She picked up the phone and dialed the numbers slowly as her heart started to race as it did when she received the prison call.

"Hello…" Monica answered.

"Hey sis, I know you have to work tomorrow but I have an emergency."

"What is it? Monica asked.

"It's Cecil. He got locked up for allegedly stealing money from his job."

"Well Sherita, you know how Cecil likes weed and he probably did. I'm not telling you what to do, but as you know, Cecil has a problem and he's not good for you. Like I told you before, you have to make that decision."

"I know sis. Please, I just need your help right now."

"How much is the bail?"

Sherita explained to her about how much the bail was to release Cecil tonight.

"Well, I can give you a hundred dollars, but I need my money back Sherita. Especially since you're borrowing it to clear his no good black ass!"

"Not a problem sis. I will definitely pay you back."

"Where or who are you going to be getting the rest of it from?

"I'm going to ask Aunt Vera. If I tell her Cecil is locked up and I need it for his bail, she won't give it to me, so I'll tell her that I need it for food. Thanks again sis! I'll call you back later."

Tonya Phillips

CHAPTER THREE

~The Perfect Couple~

D riving miles from the airport, Karen and I both were exhausted from our trip. We just got back in town from being in France for two weeks. Now it was back to the working world. Karen runs a fashion designing business and I'm an Engineer Manager. As we pulled up in front of our Victorian style, well-kept home, I had to drag our entire Louis Vuitton luggage inside because Karen was too tired. Karen parked the silver Jaguar in the garage. I left the Lexus truck at home because Karen wanted the top down on the Jag, so she can let her beautiful hair blow in the wind.

Karen and I met the winter of 1999 at a Christmas Party that my job sponsored. Two years later we got married and had an exclusive wedding, just the way Karen wanted it. There were ten bride maids, ten groomsmen, my niece Michelle was our flower girl, my nephews Javon and Delonte were the ring-bearers, and my two sisters were also included. It wasn't until soon after the wedding that Sherita changed towards Karen. I guess it was because of her situation and that coward she's involved with. Nothing surprised me when it came to my family. Especially my mother, for whom I cared for and loved so much.

Disappointed and confused at the same time, she was exposed to drugs when I was around eleven years old, after her and my father Calvin divorced. Nothing else had changed except her being in rehab. I prayed for the day she exempted herself from that abnormal way of life. I visited her from time to time, and she smiled every time she saw me. Normally, Karen would barely take the drive with me. It was an embarrassment not only for me, but for Karen as well. Mama Dorothy could never amount up to the way Karen's parents were. Her mother was a Pediatric Physician and her father, an Attorney. I would never tell Mama Dorothy that. It would only make matters worse. Not only that, me making comparisons like that would have been immature of me. I hope my family doesn't think Karen and I are more eminence than they were.

Monica is a more carefree and laid back person. I will give her that much. She takes good care of her children, goes to work, and she handles her responsibilities all by herself, although Aaron chips in every now and then.

Sherita, well let's just say she needs guidance in her life. If she can get rid of that chump that she's with, an ex-street pharmacist or should I say current, I wouldn't know. I barely talk to her or that loser she tied herself to. Not saying I don't call her, but when I do, she's always so damn private. Her problem is with Karen and I can't or don't understand why? It could just be envy. I hope the day will come when the family can get back on good terms, whenever that may be.

"Honey, sweetheart, darling, can you run me some bath water?" Karen asked Michael.

Whenever Karen needs her hubby to do something, I do it with no hesitation. I love every minute of it. Especially when she gets in the tub and I watch her beautiful body soak. When she got out, I turned off our cell phones so that I could make passionate love to my wife, the way we both love to. I pulled her body close to mine and placed my tongue in her wet vagina. Then I proceeded to stroke her long and hard, that my penis wanted to explode inside of her. Of course that was before she gently turned me over and jumped on top of me.

As she grinded my body with round motions of her hips, "Gosh! I love you. Baby this dick is so good," she whispered. After making passionate love to one another, we fell asleep in each other's arms. We didn't have to go back to work until next Tuesday anyways. We had to get prepared for the gathering in a couple of days and I wished that Mama Dorothy could make it. However, Karen didn't care if she was there or not. Although Karen doesn't clash with her family members, I understood where my wife was coming from. On the other hand, I also needed to call Monica to see if she was coming to our little shing ding as well.

"Hey sis, what's up? Karen and I just returned from our trip," he called Monica on her job.

"Hey Mike, how was France?"

"It was sensational!" He was excited. "Listen, I'm calling to see if you guys are coming to the gathering."

"Yes. I'm coming. I wouldn't miss it for anything in the world."

"And," hesitating for a bit, "what about Sherita?"

"I don't know. She's going through something right now. You know how our baby sister is."

"Yeah, tell me about it. That's always the case with her. Is it that bum again?"

Monica was a bit hesitant to say anything, knowing how he felt about Sherita's man.

"Well, Cecil got arrested the other day. He allegedly stole some money from his job."

"What? How many times have we told her about this lame ass game loser?" Michael was hot under the collar.

"She asked me to borrow two hundred dollars for his bond money and I told her that I'd give her a hundred of it, but didn't know where she would get the other half from. Aunt Vera will probably lend it to her. You know she's her favorite niece."

"That loser can't even hold onto a fast-food gig. Well, if she does come, I hope she's not planning on bringing that loser. I might have to tell him a few things like how to be a responsible man, or better yet, stay the hell away from my sister and our family. Then I'll throw him out on his ass."

With furthering his conversation with Monica, since he was already pissed behind Cecil being locked up, "Has he ever put his hands on her?"

"To be honest with you Mike, Sherita begged me not to tell you. We didn't want you to get hurt. We all know how your temper can be and we all know his track record," Monica finished.

"Who the hell cares about what he has done in the past? I'm not afraid of that punk."

"Alright, big brother. I've gotta get back to work now. I have to finish distributing this mail so I can get outta here."

"I'll see you next week. Love you sis," Michael confirmed.

By the time I got off the phone with Monica, it was four in the afternoon. I was ready for some more of Karen's loving. She was working on a scheme she was preparing and I didn't want to disturb her until after she was finished. I was horny as hell, but she looked a little tired.

"Honey," Karen called to Michael, "do you think we should wait until Mama Dorothy gets out of rehab for our celebration?"

"Baby, the invites have already gone out and it's only a week left."

"Besides, nobody knows that this is a celebration of us moving into our brand new mini mansion!" Karen's face was lit up like a light bulb.

"We'll just surprise everyone once they get here."

With a turned smirk on her face, "I just hope that Sherita doesn't come over here with that funny look she normally gives. But I'll be cordial sweetheart, don't worry. She can be snotty and evil at the same time, but I can handle her."

Saturday had arrived and everyone showed up, except for a few people. We knew that our best friends would show, in which I was very happy to see. Gabby and Janice Pearson was an established couple who lived in Columbus. Gabby was my best man at our wedding and Janice was Karen's maid of honor. Karen and Janice have known each other since the tender age of ten years old. Gabby is the owner of a prestigious construction company, and Janice is a Production Designer for the same agency where Karen works. They have two children, a son named Corey and a daughter, Jalen, which were both honor roll students.

Sherita showed up with her so-called man and Monica was accompanied by Javon and Michelle.

With a smile lit up like she won the lottery, Karen decided that it was time to announce why we were giving this party. Karen and I walked up to the DJ booth, which was on the top of our four level deck.

My beautiful wife and I proudly announced, "We are moving to an upper-grade six bedroom, four bathroom mini-mansion in Columbus."

Everyone clapped and congratulated us, except for Sherita and Cecil of course. They both just stared as though they had been hit with a hard object.

I mentioned to everyone that we weren't bragging, but just wanted to share the good news with everyone. Not to mention, I had also stepped up to a higher level in my Engineering position with a promotion from the company.

When the party was over, it was about two thirty in the morning. Some of our guests wanted to stay, but we had the DJ to announce that it was time to disburse. Cecil was crushed from all of the alcohol he had consumed. Sherita had to pick him up off the ground, he was so done. That morning, we were too tired to do anything, other than to fall asleep.

Tonya Phillips

CHAPTER FOUR

~*Mama's Dorothy's Release*~

The counselor from the rehab center entered Dorothy's room, "Miss Simmons, you have a phone call."

"Who is it?" Mama Dorothy asked.

"I believe it's your daughter Monica."

"Oh yeah, I need to talk to Meme. Thank you."

I had nicknames for all of my children. I called Sherita 'Shookie', and Mike was 'Sam' because I used to listen to *Sam Cooke* a lot when I was pregnant with him. I was listening to *'Papa's Got a Brand New Bag'* by James Brown when Monica's call came in. I'd been in here for almost two years, and will be released in one week. I promised not to use drugs ever again once I left this place. Especially if God's giving me one more chance to prove myself to the world and to my children. I had let my children down for the last time.

Shookie doesn't want anything else to do with me and I can't blame her. I just hope she doesn't hate me forever. Meme and Sam, they still love me as their mother. I know they are angry with me too and I can't blame them either. I have to find a place to live when I do get out of this place. Vera is still mad at me after all these years for what I'd done to her. I stole her money and slept with her husband. I told her in the beginning that Harold was no good for her. It still didn't make it right for what I did though. I caused major problems in this family. I know I won't be able to stay with Mike and Karen, but I'm proud of the way my children grew up, despite my actions and disoriented lifestyle.

I had done everything from marijuana, cocaine, heroin, pills, down to shooting up in my vagina. I needed to get high real fast and real quick. Getting high took a lot from me, including my family. I don't even know who Meme and Shookie's father is. I just know that Meme's father is either a guy named Percy or Wallace. With Shookie, I have no clue. I knew what they look like, but never knew their names, and I know that's why Shookie hates me so much. She never called, wrote, or came to see me.

I went to the family room to answer Meme's call, "I'm so glad to hear from you baby."

"Hey Mama Dorothy, I am too. I just called to tell you that Mike and Karen…" she was interrupted.

"What happened" I said shaking.

"Nothing mama! It's okay. It's just that they're moving into a min-mansion up in Columbus. They had a party at their house two days ago and it was really nice. They had a bar with all kinds of alcohol, wine, and beer. The DJ played all the music you wanted to hear.

"How is my daughter in law? She wasn't acting stuck up was she?"

"No mama, she was fine. Her and Mike were a little tipsy as all outdoors with drinking champagne and margarita's.

Mama Dorothy quickly changed the subject, "Are you at work Meme?"

"Yeah, but I'm coming to see you on Wednesday."

"You don't have to. I'm coming home within the next two weeks you know?"

"That's good mama. Please keep ya head up and kick this mess. It ain't worth your life or your family," Monica pleaded.

"Sherita is really mad at you. She even told me that she didn't care if you got yourself together or not, she was not dealing with you under any circumstances. I find it terrible that your own daughter doesn't want to have anything to do with you. No dealings at all mama. I forgave you and so did Mike, but if you choose to go back out there in those streets again, you will have to suffer the consequences."

Feeling the hurt in Monica's voice, she replied, "All I can say is that I'm sorry for all the pain that I put y'all through with what I've done. It's all about today now and the past is the past," she explained.

"I'm going to let you get back to work and I'll talk to you later. I need to make a phone call and see if Lefty and Bo will let me stay with them when I'm released from the center."

Lefty, Bo, and I used to get high as a kite, but I have to be strong and kick this habit. It's time I let go of this.

Once released, I stood there waiting on my bus while people were riding by in their brand new cars. Looking and staring awhile, I wished I were driving. Calvin had a nice four-door Cadillac. I can remember riding with him and Mike down to the park with no worries and no struggles. He was a good father to Mike, taking him everywhere he went. Most of the time, I stayed at home washing clothes and cooking dinner. We were happy then. I often wondered what happened, then realized that it was me that destroyed my whole life in the process.

As I waited, the bus pulled up just before I finished my cigarette. I smashed it on the ground and I got on. When I got off the bus, Lefty and Bo were standing on the front porch drinking a beer. They stared at me as though they saw a ghost.

"Damn Dot," they use to call me, "you gained some weight. You look good though. You want a beer?"

"No, I'll pass."

"What? You scared you might get back on the wagon or something?"

"Damn Bo, you should have drank that shit before I got here if you were a friend."

"You gotta be strong Dot," Bo replied.

"I am strong. That's why I told you NO!"

Bo and Lefty were from back in the day when we used to get high together. I mean real high.

"Dot you look sick," Lefty mentioned.

30

"Drugs don't make nobody lose that much weight," Bo followed.

"Don't pay Lefty any mind. His ass is drunk. Did you take a HIV test?"

"Sure did! I had to after going into the center. It was required."

"Especially with the way we shared needles together," Bo said.

I knew that Bo also liked men. He was always telling people how he used to bust ass. I had something to be scared of, and I knew it. But I never confessed to my children. Most of the time, we were in the smoke house. The faggots would come over and give Bo heroin because he said it made his dick real hard. Bo would use them for money to get his dope. I watched Bo and Lefty the whole time while they drank beer and liquor from each other, without touching one single cup.

"I will take it one day at a time and everything will be okay. Me and my children will become close again," Mama Dorothy added.

Tonya Phillips

CHAPTER FIVE

~Monica's Trip~

Lavern and I planned to take our kids to Disneyland for our summer vacation, which will be my first time riding on a plane. Lavern had flown many times before. I'm a bit frightened, but I'll get used to it. Michelle and Javon were very excited. I was happy that my children were going to enjoy themselves. This will be their first time going somewhere fun. I wish I could take my nephew Delonte, but Sherita would have had to pay for his airline ticket. I know that's almost impossible, considering the bind she'd put herself into, especially with that no good Cecil getting his dumb ass in trouble with his job. He didn't make much money anyway. She was practically paying all the bills on her own salary. I wouldn't pay for nothing. I'd let his ass suffer all the pain he put her through. I hated to have to leave Delonte, but I would have ended up having to spank his spoil ass. I'll call her anyway to see if she could give me at least sixty dollars towards half of his ticket.

"Hello Sherita, I'm going on my vacation in a couple of weeks from now. Lavern and I are taking the kids to Disneyland, and I wanted to know if you could spare sixty dollars for half on Delonte's airfare. I wanted to take him with us too."

"Oh that's nice. I get paid next Thursday, so I can get it to you then if that's fine. When are y'all leaving?"

"We're leaving the Friday after next. So Thursday will be fine with me. I'll go ahead and pay for it tomorrow and you just reimburse me, okay? I want all of my money Sherita, not half, but all!" Monica said in a stern voice.

"I know. I owe you anyway."

"Yes, that's right!"

"So I will be giving you one hundred and sixty dollars."

Sherita kept defending that man for whatever reason. She'll see and when she does, I hope it won't be too late. I didn't want anything to happen to her. She just had to have a man in her bed. We as women have to stop sugar coating things and start realizing what's really going on and important. Especially when we feel we are being taking advantage of.

"So, what is Cecil doing now?"

"Nothing! He said he would start looking for a job on Monday."

"I suppose he's depending on your money right now, huh?" I said angrily.

"I don't give Cecil money. Since he lost his job for being stupid, he won't have shit."

"So he really stole that money?"

"I think so," Sherita confirmed.

"Uuuhh...," hesitating to herself, Monica added, "I also mentioned to Mike that Cecil had hit you before."

"Why the hell did you do that? You know if he would've known, not only would I have been paying his bail money to get his ass out of jail, but I would've been paying for his hospital bills too. Speaking of our brother did you hear that shit at the party?"

"What shit? About the house?"

"Yeah!" Why would they move into a six bedroom house and it's only the two of them?" Sherita asked with an attitude.

"I'm happy for them myself."

"I knew you would be."

"You're always talking negative about them. Somebody in this family needs to have some class and style, so why not?

Sherita turned a bit quiet and then stated, "You have to admit, they think they're better than anyone in this family."

Sherita's attitude changed when she decided to switch the subject of Mike and Karen, as she always does when the conversation doesn't go her way.

"I bought Delonte some summer outfits. I will start packing his stuff now."

"You're so excited as if you're going."

"I wish the hell I was going with y'all, but I can't afford it right now, and you know this."

With a sarcastic remark, "What and leave Cecil? He would hit the ceiling if he knew you were leaving his ass here in Cleveland to go on a vacation."

"Hold on one minute, my other line is clicking." Monica answered her other line, but clicked back over, "Sherita, let me call you back, it's Lavern."

"Okay, I have to pack Delonte's things anyway."

Monica continued her conversation with Lavern about their trip. Both were very excited about it and couldn't wait 'til the day came for them to leave. They talked about how people were asking for souvenirs, and they hadn't even stepped foot on the plane yet.

"Girl, I'm so glad that you called. I'm so tired to talking to Sherita about Cecil, it's not even funny anymore. Now he doesn't have a job and Sherita's always defending him, knowing he was wrong for what he did."

"Is he looking for work?" Lavern asked.

"Nope. And it looks as though as he won't be looking for a job any time soon. He's constantly begging Sherita's ass. If anything, I think he's just so ridiculous that it makes no sense."

"Well, that's Sherita for you. How long have they been dating?" Lavern asked.

"They've been together for about five years too long. It's the same ole tired bullshit. I'm worried about her Lavern. I can't do anything but worry."

After talking on the phone for about thirty minutes or so, Mama Dorothy showed up at my door. As I looked out of the peep hole, I wondered who left the door open to the building that had a security lock on it. She looks as though as she put on a little bit of weight.

"Hey Meme," Dorothy said gladly after the door opened, "I just came to visit you today," she confirmed.

I was glad to see her, but she wasn't staying here with me. I was afraid she'd start using again. I pray that she doesn't, but you never know.

"Where are you staying? With Bo and Lefty? You know they're trouble. Why don't you stay in a women's shelter?" Monica asked.

"They are full. I called before I left the center."

"Mama, you've been drinking too," she said disappointed.

"I had one beer Meme."

"Damn mama, I hope it wasn't anything else because trust me, I'm cutting all contact with you if it were." I meant every word of what I said to her.

"Where you going with all of this luggage in the living room?" Mama asked looking around Monica's place.

"My friend Lavern and I are going to Disneyland. We're taking the kids and Delonte too."

"So, when are y'all leaving?" Mama inquired.

"We're leaving on Friday."

Mama Dorothy thought about it, but not for long, when she blurted out, "well, you should let me crash here until y'all get back."

"I can't do that right now mama," I told her while walking towards the kitchen.

"And why not?" Mama shouted.

"Because mama, you just got out and I don't want to have to worry about things while I'm gone. That's too much pressure on me right now."

"Worrying about what things? Are you talking about your personal things being gone?" Mama Dorothy headed for the front door with her head held high, "I'll let you go then."

"I'll call you when I get back. Do they have a phone in that house where you are staying?" Monica asked before Mama left the apartment.

"Not yet. Bo said he will call the phone company next week to get the phone turned on."

Lavern, the kids, and I promptly arrived at the airport with tons of luggage. After boarding the plane and getting comfortable, we laid back and relaxed for the ride. When we arrived in Florida, the sun was beaming and it was a beautiful day. We checked into our hotel and it was nice and lovely. The only thing Delonte kept talking about, with his hyper ass, was getting on the rides. After we made sure our luggage was together and put away, we went to eat at a restaurant down in the lobby of the hotel. The kids were hungry from the flight, and so were Lavern and I. Her two boys can eat! They always had healthy appetites.

After eating and resting awhile, we made our way to the park. We rode the rides for damn near almost five hours in the hot ass sun. Then we headed to the wave pool to cool ourselves off a bit. It seemed like everybody and their grand mamma were here in Florida.

I enjoyed the fact that I finally got a chance to show off my thick beautiful legs. It's been three days and it was very exciting. We still had four days left and we planned to make the best of it. At least I was.

I wish we had a chance to come to Florida when we were younger, but Mama Dorothy let herself be first and neglected us. Drugs were her first priority, not us. I watched the kids enjoy themselves, and I still couldn't believe we were here. We took many pictures so that we'd have memories and my kids would be able to share something with their children someday perhaps. As I sat there on the side of the pool, I kept having negative thoughts about my relationships with Aaron, but I soon realized that I was on vacation!

The next day we took the kids to a parade and then let them get on the rides again at the park. After that, Lavern and I decided to go to this place where we noticed a lot of couples sitting. They were holding hands, kissing, and hugging. Looking at each other, we both wished someone was holding and kissing us that same way.

"You see all these people out here carrying on?" Lavern asked.

"Yeah, sure do," I said.

Feeling a bit sad, "Okay, we need to get away from this part of the park."

"I'm with you Lavern. Let's take the kids to the Universal Studios."

This was the last day of the trip. We were exhausted and tired after we left the studios. We ended up sleeping practically the rest of the day.

The next morning, we started packing up.

"*I wished it wasn't over so soon*," I thought to myself.

"The next time we are going to Jamaica just you and I," Lavern suggested.

"Sounds like a plan to me."

I was all with Lavern's plan, but in reality, I really hope to have a man by then. If that happens, I will be taking him with me wherever that may be.

We spent most of our morning gathering our things together so that we could leave the hotel in time to catch a shuttle back to the airport. We were all tired, including the kids, and couldn't wait to return home safely. Once the plane arrived back home at the airport, we gathered our things, said our goodbye's for the evening, got into our cars, and drove off.

CHAPTER SIX

~*Club Night with Sherita*~

F*amily Affair* was playing by Mary J. Blige, the club was jumping, and I couldn't stop dancing. I danced so much that I was drenched with sweat, and I knew Champagne was sweaty, as heavy as she was. She's my friend and all, but when we went out, we made the best of it. We were having a good time until two guys got into a fight over a spilled drink. Didn't they hear what Mary's song was about?

"*I swear, people don't know how to have fun anymore,*" I thought to myself. However, the bouncers threw their asses out too.

"Men are the ones always causing most of the fights."

"Only some of them Sherita, not all of them!" Champagne replied.

"I'm still glad to be out tonight. Especially with getting away from Cecil. I'm so tired of handling all of the responsibilities. I have to take care of my son too!" Sherita started to vent. "Now he done up and lost his job and all of the burdens are on me."

Champagne continued to nod her head, agreeing with what Sherita was talking about while sipping on her Alize', "And all he can do is smoke weed and drink. I'm ready to get rid of his ass. You know what I mean girl?"

Waiting for a verbal response this time from Champagne, she replied, "I say let him go! I mean, that's your choice. I can't tell you what to do. I have five kids and five baby daddies, and neither one of them help me. If it wasn't for my mother, I don't know what I would do.

"Well, Delonte's father is locked up for the next ten years. Hell, when he get out, Delonte will be nineteen years old. I'm not going to keep him away from his father, but I will let him know that I carried all the struggles and burdens by myself. He has no say so on a damn thing right now. I really hope that Delonte makes it in life, because his father won't get to share none of it."

Champagne stood up from her seat. "I'll be back…," she was a little short.

"Hold up, where are you going?"

"I'm going over here to the bar. You see that guy staring at me with his fine ass? He got the dreads all fresh, a nice outfit. I'm going over there so he can buy me a drink."

Sherita laughed, "and you betta bring your ass back here too. Don't do nothing I won't do!"

"Girl please!" Champagne said before heading off to the bar. "I'm going to get this drink and bring my ass back here so we can have some more fun."

It had been two and a half hours since Champagne went to the bar. I looked all over the club for her and I was getting worried that something had went wrong. What if she got raped or he killed her? I didn't wanna think negative, but I just hoped that she was okay. I will definitely give her a piece of my mind when I do catch up with her though.

I waited until the lights came on and there was still no sign of Champagne. It would have been nice if her mother had let her borrow the car, but she knows how Champagne gets when she's been out drinking. Considering she has kids she still has to raise. It was about a quarter to four in the morning now and here I was standing out here in 'no man's land' waiting on a cab, while she's got her legs gapped open in some raggedy ass hotel somewhere. I had a pretty good idea that she went with that guy to have sex tonight. I waited for a cab until this guy pulled up in a green Chevy Blazer and ask me what my name was.

"What's your name baby?" The guy yelled through the passenger side window.

"It's Sherita," I answered back.

"Do you need a ride?"

"No, I was waiting for my girlfriend. But it seems she left me, so I'm waiting on a cab and when I do talk to her, I'm going to get in her ass for real."

"Don't beat the sister down," he said trying to bring a smile to the frown that I'd displayed.

"I'm just mad right now. She knew she shouldn't have done that crap."

"So you're telling me that she left you out here alone?"

"Yeah, that's what I'm saying and neither one of us drive, so we caught a cab down here."

"Damn, y'all were pressed to come clubbing tonight, huh?"

"You can say that. She was more ready to go than I was.

"Oh, by the way, my name is R. Kelly," he joked and then corrected himself, "I'm just kidding sweetheart. My name is Nathan."

With a small grin upon my face, "well, it's nice to meet you Nathan, but I really do need to get home."

He turned off his truck and exited to come around to talk to me, instead of talking through the window.

"I'll take you home. I won't bite."

"I know you won't bite 'cause I'll bite yo ass back," she laughed.

I looked him up and down with his nice haircut, light brown cocoa skin, and his somewhat baggie jeans, and a pair of Jordan tennis shoes and thought to myself, "*Just like I like them, well groomed and handsome.*"

"No seriously, I'll take you home."

"I can't. I have a boyfriend and he's probably worried and going crazy like he normally does, wondering where I am right now.

"Oh...you didn't tell him you were going to a club?"

"No I didn't. He has a temper!"

"Then, you don't need him. I promise I'll drop you off around the corner then."

"Okay, I guess so. I just hope he doesn't come outside looking," I said almost trembling.

Faces Of Shame

After giving him the address in which I needed to go, I stepped up into his truck and it smelled of fresh fruit and cologne. We sat and talked until about five that morning. I confided in him, a complete stranger, about the problems Cecil and I were having, which was a major mistake because most men seem to use that against you later on.

It got so bad that I needed some Kleenex. As he handed me the tissue, he rubbed my back and said, "Don't worry Sherita, it will be okay."

I looked him up and down again and he placed his hand on my thigh. I wanted to tell him no, but my lips wouldn't allow me to. I moved my leg as I kept thinking about Cecil. Here I was outside with another man, in his truck, and I have one sitting at home worried to death. In a way, I didn't care. Especially with the way he had been acting lately. Not helping me with the household, or the bills for that matter. On top of all that, he lost his damn job. I hope like hell he was worried.

"Nathan. I think you should take me home now."

"Okay, it's no problem," he started up his truck.

From that moment, I just knew I was going to end up in the news dead at twenty three years old from being raped, stabbed, or shot. Before he put the truck in drive, he leaned over towards me and we started tongue kissing, which led to us ending up in a hotel room, which he'd paid for. I was hoping he wouldn't ask me for any money, because I didn't have any.

Once in the room, we kissed and kissed. The kisses began to get more and more intense. He then knelt down between my legs, slowly removed my panties down to my ankles, and laid me down on the bed.

45

Spreading my legs open wide, he kissed me all the way up my thighs until his manhood was deep inside of me. I wanted to scream at first. He pressed against my vaginal walls so hard, I was spellbound. I kept grinding my hips against his. He was moaning and so was I. It was as though we were in love or something and I didn't know this man at all.

"What the hell am I doing?" I kept asking myself. Part of me felt guilty after it was over, but it felt so good. Nathan and I just stared at each other. After it was all over, my cell phone kept ringing. I looked down at it and it was Cecil. I couldn't bare it anymore. Nathan was a better lover than Cecil was in the bedroom. He was well endowed. We went at it again and the more my phone rung, the sex got more intense. This time he performed oral sex. It was to the point of no return.

Afterwards, he called me a cab and gave me cab fare to get home. It was my idea, because I didn't want to put him in the middle of my drama after the night we just had. It was about eleven in the morning and I knew Cecil was going to hit the roof.

As I sat there in the hotel room waiting on the cab, I felt so bad about my deceit with Cecil, although I knew he was no good.

"What's wrong baby?" Nathan asked.

"I just feel a little guilty, that's all."

"Why? You said he don't treat you right."

"I know, but I love him and I don't know anything about you. All I know is your name."

"Well, I apologize Sherita. It's Washington. That's my last name. I have no wife, no kids, nor a girlfriend. I'm outright single. I live with a Muslim roommate and his name is Saleem.

"You're probably calling me all kinds of names in your head right about now, huh?" Sherita added.

"No. We're grown right?"

"Yeah, but it happened the first night."

I had the nerve to be thinking negative about Champagne and here I was, doing the same thing.

"If you need to talk, I'm here," Nathan said.

"Well, I have a son and his name is Delonte and he can be just a bit spoiled."

"Well, maybe we can go play ball sometimes, would you like that?"

Sherita sat for a minute before answering, "Yes I would. I would really like that."

Most men don't bother with women after they have sex with them. Especially not with a one night stand.

The cab finally showed up in the parking lot and he walked me to the car.

"Call me later?" I asked him as he started to get into his truck that was parked in the next spot.

"Of course I will Sherita," he blew me a kiss.

As I got in the house, Cecil was lying on the couch smoking weed as usual. His feet smelled up the whole apartment. Like always, he jumped up from his seat, "where the fuck you been Sherita?"

"I was out with Champagne."

"Oh, at the fucking club right?"

Balling up his fist as to get ready to hit me, "it's the next fuckin' morning and you think I'm gonna buy that bullshit coming from you? If I find out you been fuckin some other bitch ass nigga, you're a dead bitch!" He swore to me. "And, who the fuck told you to go to the club anyway? It damn sure wasn't me!"

I turned around slowly, gaining confidence in myself for once, "I don't remember you being my father Cecil. I don't need permission to go anywhere."

Yelling out of his own frustration, "Your fuckin sister called here asking me when you were picking up Delonte. And your boogey ass brother called too. I just need to get away from this wanna-be ass family and take my ass back to the Bronx. I've been thinking about going back there anyway."

"Then maybe that's what you should you do. You can't seem to make it out here in Cleveland," I replied.

"Shut up you crazy ass bitch!" He yelled.

"I'm calling my sister."

Rushing towards me to snatch the phone from my hand, "you ain't callin' nobody," he said.

"Leave me alone Cecil."

"Tell me where the fuck you been!"

"It's none of your fuckin' business where I've been!"

Cecil took his fist and hit me numerous of times in the face, which knocked me out for a bit. I woke up later that morning with a black eye. My face was all bruised up.

"*I don't know why I didn't call the police*," I thought to myself. I was so mad at Cecil and I know now that I have to let him go. I got so frustrated with him not motivating himself that I cheated on him.

I finally thought about all that I'd been through with Cecil, with him not giving all that he could anymore to this relationship, not to mention him beating on me, and grabbed all of Cecil's clothes and threw them off of the balcony.

"What the hell are you doing Sherita?"

"I'm throwing out your shit!"

"I ain't going nowhere…," he said with confidence.

He started to come towards me again in an angry rage so that he could finish the job he'd done on me earlier. After he'd finished hitting me again and again, I waited until he left the room and called the police. When they arrived, they didn't have to ask any questions and I didn't have to answer any, and they placed him under arrest. The only words that needed to be spoken were the bruises on my face, which told the entire story alone.

CHAPTER SEVEN

~*Drop In The bucket*~

It was two thirty in the morning and there were stems, beer cans, Brandy bottles, and needles all over the place. I knew it was a mistake staying here with them all night long. I smoked cocaine from sun up to sun down. Bo and Lefty were more zipped out than I was. I felt bad and sad at the same time. I especially felt unreliable to my family. I can beat my own ass for doing this shit again.

Here I am, fifty years old. I constantly asked myself, "*when will this madness come to an end?*"

It was such a shame and a waste. I'd be better off dead, if the drugs don't take me first. I had a headache and was vomiting. I was just outright sick. I couldn't call MeMe and tell her or my son about how I was feeling. They both would cut me out of their lives for good.

Shooky already hated me and I couldn't change the way she felt. I starting thinking that maybe I should go back into rehab. I wasted practically my whole entire life bouncing around in and out of drug treatment facilities. I'm the one who had to stop starving and eat.

I got tired of just laying around. So I got up, went into the bathroom to wash my face, and there Bo was, tightening a plastic rope around his arm and injecting dope into his veins.

"Come on Dot, I need some privacy. Either you're gonna get some of this shit or shut the fuckin door."

Not being able to resist after all of the thinking that I'd just done, "Just a little Bo, I'm trying real hard to kick this shit. I don't want to keep disappointing my kids."

"You a grown ass woman ain't you?"

"Yeah, I'm a grown woman," Dorothy replied.

"Well, take this shit and enjoy it!"

I loved shooting heroin. It helped make me forget about everything I thought about or would think about. But, after the injection, I still had a headache.

Bo started using drugs at the age of fifteen and still uses at forty-six. He was always doing underhanded shit. He was always scheming, conniving, and stealing. The reason he's here in Ohio now is because he did some crooked shit back in Washington, DC, which is where he's from, stealing drugs from the drug dealers there. So far he's been lucky because, he's been here for over ten years or so now.

I can remember the time when he told Lefty and I that he was having sex with his male friend in his mother's basement. Bo was more gay than bi-sexual. He claimed he's been with hundreds of women. The way that he talks to people, you can tell he's gay. I'm surprised he hasn't caught AIDS by now. His baby sister is a lesbian, and wears her pants hanging off of her ass like most of the men do these days. She wears men clothing, and sports a close haircut. His brother Andre, is a Trans-Sexual.

He carries purses and has a long hair weave. The word on the street is that Andre has the virus. I don't know how true it is, but it will come out sooner or later.

Andre calls himself *Cynthia.* He would never answer anybody if they call him Andre. Although Bo dresses like a man, he is more in the closet with his sex life than anything. Lefty and I know the truth though.

Lefty is a cocaine smoker and an alcoholic. He can drink a half gallon of Bacardi every other day. Both Lefty and Bo get disability checks every month. I don't know how they pull that shit off because they're both able to work. They do side jobs for people in the neighborhood, so that's how they're getting their ends.

Lefty is from Cleveland. He and Bo met when they were buying dope on one of the most notorious streets of Ohio. From that point on, they have been friends ever since. I just happened to be in the area whoring and tricking, whatever you wanna call it. I didn't care about anything or anybody, not even my own children. All I wanted to do is get high real quick and real fast.

Lefty and I went to the store to get some corn meal to fry some fish one day. We wanted some grits with it as well. I had twelve dollars and Lefty had six. We spent most of our money on drugs earlier. I had to get the twelve dollars from Bo because I had no income. I only got food stamps every month.

"Dot, why don't you buy that shit with your food stamps and save this money? Then we can buy some beer."

I knew in my mind Lefty wanted to buy some drugs. I kept the twelve dollars because tomorrow I was getting my ass up and out to look for a job. It was something I should have been doing in the first place when I got out of rehab. That way, I could have rented a room until I got on my feet.

When Lefty and I got back to the boarding house from the store, Lefty was screaming, "Hurry, hurry! Dot, get up here!"

"What happened?" I asked while looking down at Bo, who was lying on the floor with a needle still in his arm. He was cold and dead. He'd overdosed on heroin. It was almost the worst thing that I've ever experienced in my life. It was from that moment on that I had to surrender from this awful lifestyle that I've endured.

When I was married to Mike's father, I had it all. He took care of his responsibilities like a man should have. I finished high school and had a seemingly good life. I had a supporting husband, good kids, and a nice home. Then I went down to poverty, drugs, and not a damn penny to my name. I asked for this shit. I wasn't forced into this life. I chose to be this way. The drugs were so good that I couldn't help myself. I blamed my longtime friend Edna at first. She had it bad and sold everything she owned. She had nine children and some of them are now on drugs.

One day she asked me to snort some cocaine with her and like a damn fool, I did. I liked it from that point on and have been dipping in this shit ever since.

When the ambulance and the coroner arrived, they put Bo's fragile body in a black body bag and carried it out. His funeral was a week later and everyone who knew him from D.C., New York, New Jersey, and Ohio were there. The funeral home was jammed packed with having barely anyplace to sit. Tears fell from everyone's eyes, they were so heart broken. We had been through so much together that Lefty and I still couldn't believe that Bo was now gone.

I didn't call Meme about Bo's death because she really didn't know him. If she knew that I slipped up and relapsed, she would never talk to me again, just like Shookie.

Bo's mother just stared into space after walking up to the casket. It was so sad that she'd lost her son to drugs. She was eighty-five years old and she out-lived her own child. As the saying goes, '*the parents aren't supposed to outlive the kids*', but they are now a days.

She was disappointed of her kids. She had three just as I did. But instead, my kids were doing fine and their mother was the one who disappointed them.

After the autopsy was done on Bo, his sister told us that not only was his death caused by the heroin, but he was also HIV positive as well, which really made my stomach turn. I started shaking after remembering sharing a needle with him that day. Lefty and I looked at each other and fell into each other's arms and broke down once again.

After hearing that bit of information and looking back on our drug lives, Lefty and I knew that we had to seriously make a decision on changing our lives now. Lefty said that he was going to get himself together and he meant it. Two weeks later, I packed up and moved out. I started looking for work and stayed at a shelter.

"*I don't know who's going to hire me at age fifty, but anything will do at this point,*" is what I thought to myself every day. When Lefty said that he was getting himself together, so was I. I was determined that I was getting my family back, no matter what it took! And 'til this day, Lefty and I both hadn't used now for over a month.

CHAPTER EIGHT

~*More Drama*~

The drive on the beltway was congested as usual. I was on my way to drop Delonte's spoiled ass back off to Sherita. I don't know why she hasn't been over to pick him up yet, but I'm a bit worried, but that's the courtesy that I get. She's so stupid when it comes to that loser, as Mike would call him. Sometimes I wish I knew somebody to knock his ass off, but then again, he's not worth it. That means I'll end up in jail and lose everything I've worked so hard for. Sherita has to make a choice on whether to leave that dog or stay with his low- life ass.

While driving, Delonte was in the back crying because we went to the store and he wanted some ice cream, but wouldn't let him have it. Sherita would always let him have his way, but not with me. I'm not the one. As he kept crying, I pulled over and spanked his ass and made him shut up after that old fashioned ass whooping.

The traffic was still hectic.

"*Damn,*" I thought to myself, "*I'm never getting out of this traffic jam or over to Sherita's.*"

I prayed all the way there, hoping nothing had happened to my only sister. I sat there for another fifteen minutes trying to get off of this beltway. As I turned onto her street and into the complex, a police cruiser was leaving out of the neighborhood. Now I was really worried and was wondering what the hell went down. Something was always going on around here. She needed to move and I told her a thousand times to get the hell away from the area. Either someone was getting hurt, or the dope boys were selling their products outside of the buildings anywhere they could.

That's why I moved from that ghetto ass neighborhood. It seemed like everybody was dysfunctional in some kind of way, shape, or form. The kids had no role models in their lives, neither mother nor father. I really wish that she would move. If it wasn't for Cecil's lazy game playing, unmotivated ass, she probably would have moved. She claimed the rent was reasonable and that she only pays five hundred and fifty dollars a month, which is very cheap these days. If Cecil would just get off of his lazy ass, she would have more help. Hell, I pay a thousand dollars a month, which is a little steep for me, but I keep my head above water.

As I knocked on the door, no one answered until about three minutes later when I heard her say, "Wait a minute. Who is it?"

"It's me…I'm bringing Delonte home. What's taking you so long to open the door? It's hot in this damn hallway and your son's irritability is starting to get on my damn nerves. I already had to pull over on the highway to spank that ass, so come on and open this damn door," I yelled.

"Mommy, I want some ice cream," Delonte' said through the door.

"Boy shut up, she's coming!"

"Sherita, you got less than two minutes to open this damn door, or I will leave his ass out here in this hot ass hallway."

"Don't do that Monica…," Sherita yelled as she made her way to unlock the door. When she finally opened the door, she had a towel wrapped around her face.

Snatching the towel from her face, "What the hell happened to you? Where is that muthafuckin' Cecil at?" I asked out of anger.

"They just locked him up for domestic violence."

"His ass already in trouble and then he does this to you?"

"I have to go to court to testify about his job."

"But you don't have anything to do with his ass stealing that money," I told her.

"No, I don't really."

"Well, I'm gonna tell you like this, if you go back to him or go to court for him, I'm not speaking to you anymore and I mean it. Just like you don't want to have anything to do with Mama Dorothy, it will be the same way for you. And speaking of Mama Dorothy, did I tell you she got out of rehab?"

"No, and I don't care if she did. That lazy bitch is sickening. I can't stand her ass."

"Well, I'm calling Mike to tell him what Cecil did to you."

"And what is he going to do? He's going to talk the same shit he's been talking."

"What the hell did he hit you for anyway?" I asked her, pulling her by the shoulders towards me.

Sherita explained the situation about her going out to the club with Champagne the night before and not letting him know, and how she didn't have to check in with anybody because he wasn't her father, nor her husband. Then she talked about how good of a time they were having and when Champagne left the table, she didn't come back from the bar where some dude had brought her a drink.

"You know you can't hang out with Champagne. She's a slut and you know that. She barely takes care of those five kids. She leaves them with her mother all the time. I really hope you learned your lesson about going out with her again."

"I haven't even heard from her yet, so I don't know where she is."

"Well, I'm about to go, but I'm going to call you later. Get some rest and don't let his ass back in here Sherita. I'm serious!" I stated once again as I exited the front door of the apartment.

I prayed from the time I left Sherita's place until I got home. Hoping and wishing that they wouldn't let that bum out for him to come back and hurt my sister. After reaching the house, my phone kept ringing and it was a number that I didn't recognize, but I answered it anyway. I thought it may have been somebody I met at the post office. The last person I met was an idiot. He didn't take me out, there were no flowers, and all he wanted was some pussy and I kept it moving. But when I picked up the call, it was Mama Dorothy and she sounded really sad. I knew she would call with some sob ass story.

"Hey Meme, just wanted to tell you that Bo died. I know that you didn't know him, but he was one of my friends I used to get high with."

"Oh, well I'm sorry to hear that. When did he die?"

"Well, it's been almost a month now."

"Why didn't you call me? I would have gone to the funeral, even though I didn't know him. I mean, you told me about them before, but I would have been there to give you some support."

"I was too embarrassed to call you. I fell overboard ..."

Starting to get frustrated, "can you stop with all the beating around the bush talking?" I knew she had started using drugs again, but I wanted her to tell me.

"I got weak and started using drugs again. I didn't mean to hurt you. Please don't hang up. They were trying to push the drugs on me, but I didn't wanna use again, and I was too helpless. I felt that I had no other choice in the matter being around the stuff. I got hungry and I needed to be fed."

"What do you mean you had no choice in the matter?"

"I'm sorry Meme but drugs are a hard thing to kick, especially when you've used them. But after seeing Bo in that casket and learning that he had AIDS, that made me change my prospective on my life. I know I let y'all down, but I will make up for it."

"Well I hope so because I'm tired of going through problems with this family. Sherita got herself in some mess with Cecil again."

"What happened," Dorothy asked.

"Cecil blacked her eye and busted her lip because she went to the club with Champagne the other night. He's an asshole and I told Sherita to leave Cecil's no good ass."

"Oh no! This is all my fault. If I would have been there, this would not have happened."

"No mama, even if you were here it would have happened. Sherita is the cause of her own happiness and unfortunately, she loves that piece of shit of a man."

"He is a piece shit and I have to agree with you on that. I promise I will make y'all love me again. All three of you!" Mama Dorothy reclaimed. "I love all of you unconditionally, and nothing means more to me than to have y'all back in my life."

"Well, I pray every day mama. I pray that we can become a close knit family again. I would love to talk to you more right now, but I'm on my way back over to Sherita's house and then I have to go grocery shopping before I go to work tomorrow."

"Before you hang up…" Dorothy had one more question, "how's Aaron doing?"

"He's fine. He still picks the kids up when he can."

Mama and I ended our phone conversation, but not before letting me know that she had an interview at a doctor's office on Hefner Street in a couple of days.

As I pulled up in front of the building, there was a strong and unpleasant smell of urine that lingered in the hallway. Once I got to the door, Delonte was quick to open it.

I had told him once before about just opening the door. I mean, it could have anybody or even that scum ass Cecil.

"I knew it was you Auntie!"

"I don't care! You don't open the door like that." I told him while pointing in his face. I sent Michelle and Javon to the back room because it was too much going on to send the kids outside.

Continuing the conversation from me being there earlier, Sherita explained from the beginning how everything between her and Cecil had transpired. She talked about how she was waiting on Champagne while sitting at the table, sipping on her Mocha. Barely holding back a tear and looking at my sister's face, I thought for a minute, "*I wish I had a gun. I'd blow his head clean the fuck off.*"

Sherita continued her story, "So when she didn't come back, I was still waiting on a cab. This guy pulled up in a green Chevy Blazer and told me his name was Nathan. We talked for a good little while, and then we ended up going to the hotel afterwards. We made love and it wasn't just sex, like me and Cecil normally had."

"Hell, I'm glad you went out and fucked somebody else. Maybe you can get over this bastard and move on with your life. So tell me about this Nathan character. Have you talked to him today?" I asked, wanting to know more about the juicy details. Does he know about that simple ass Cecil?"

"Yeah, I told Nathan everything about his sorry ass."

"And how does he feel about it?"

"I guess he's okay with it. He really didn't say much."

I had to really see where Sherita's head was at, so I asked, "So are you going to get back with Cecil or what?"

"I doubt that seriously. If he gets himself together…"

"Oh please," interrupting Sherita's next sentence, "as though that will happen. When you met Cecil, what you saw is what you got."

"Okay, I'm not going back to him sis," Sherita said with her head hung low.

"I hope the hell not because he's not worth the headache or pain." Now switching the subject off of Cecil, "Mama Dorothy has an interview with this doctor's office in a few days."

"That lady needs something to do with her life," Sherita mumbled.

"Sherita, you are so mean when it comes to Mama Dorothy. But I can't be mad at you though. You have a right to be upset with her. I clearly understand how you feel about the situation. So how was it with Nathan?"

Sounding very excited, "Girl, it was the absolute best!"

"I wish I can get me some," I said as I was getting up from the couch and getting the kids to get ready to head out again, "I'm about to burst. This pussy ain't been touched in so long that I'm almost scared to go to the doctor and have an exam done."

Laughing together as they once did some years ago, Sherita leaned over and gave me a hug and a kiss on the cheek, as well as hugs to the kids before we all left.

CHAPTER NINE

~What Happened in Vegas?~

Karen and I wanted to go to Vegas for a few days to get away from the work that was wearing our bodies out, although it was back to work until we moved into our new home. Once we got to Las Vegas, went to the hotel where we reserved a suite, way up on the twenty sixth floor. We put up our luggage, which were genuine leather, with matching briefcases. I'm not sure on why we even brought briefcases. This was the reason for our get-a-way in the first place. We weren't there do any work, just fun and love making for the short time that we'd planned to be here. We were so exhausted from the plane ride that we didn't feel much like doing anything.

"Baby, I need a massage." Karen gestured, but I really wanted to relax.

"This massage will make you sleepy and when you wake up, I have a surprise for you."

I gave her a massage and let my baby get some rest. I knew she needed it. She does so much at her job with sketching materials for the company. My job required a lot of my time as well, but I went to the gift shop in the lobby to get some roses for my beautiful wife. Then I decided to go to the casino, although I wasn't much of a gambler. I played a few slots and got on the Black Jack table where I lost a few bucks, got up from the table and just walked around some. As I was sitting there playing the slots, I noticed this woman looking at me, but then as I got a closer look at her face, I noticed she was a Transsexual. She, or shall I say he, kept staring at me, then he spoke.

"How are you?" he asked me.

"I'm fine," I replied as if I didn't notice that *she* was a *he*.

"So can I ask, how much money did you lose?"

"Sure, it's not a problem. I just lost a little, not much."

"I don't like losing money," he started a conversation.

"Well I don't gamble much either. I just do it for fun."

"So, where are you from?"

They continued to engage in conversation, which led to Michael telling him that he was from Cleveland, Ohio and was a married man. Then I asked why there were so many questions, but never got an answer. I rose from my seat and headed towards the bathroom and the guy followed and watched as I went into one of the stalls.

When I came out of the stall, the guy was just standing there. Then he approached me, got on his knees, and unzipped my jeans. At first I was stunned, but then he started giving me a hella fide blowjob. I had always been curious as to how it would feel to be with another man.

After it was over, I felt a little ashamed, embarrassed, and guilty as hell. Karen couldn't find out about this and I had to make sure of that. I don't know what the fuck I was thinking about. This was going to be my little secret. There was no way in hell that I could let this cat out of the bag.

My cell phone started ringing and while reaching for my cell phone, I wondered, *"Who could this be? I'm trying to enjoy the rest of my vacation and I knew that Karen was asleep,"* but it was Monica.

"Hey sis, what are you up too? Is something wrong?" I asked her since she'd called me so late in the night.

"Everything is wrong. It's Mama Dorothy and Sherita. They need help!" She sounded a bit depressed. "I have mama on the phone too," she informed him.

"Hey mama!" I said with excitement in my voice.

"How is my son and where are you?"

"Karen and I are in Las Vegas."

"You and Karen living the good life, huh?" Mama Dorothy asked yet another question.

"We try to. When you work as hard as we do, that's the luxury and the comfort of it all."

"Well baby…I just wanted to tell you that I'm out of drug treatment now and trying to get back on my feet. I want us to be a family again, just like it used to be."

"How are you feeling mama?" I asked her.

Mama Dorothy went on to tell him how she'd lost one of her friends due to an overdose of heroin. She tried to hold back, but also continued to tell him how she'd slipped up and started back using before

69

Bo's death and how she was now going to get it together this one last time. His death really made her see the light this time. She had realized that she had to be the one to get her life in order, without being in anyone's treatment center.

"Oh no. I should have known with you being around those good for nothing people anyway."

"Baby, I had nowhere else to go and I couldn't stay with my kids. Especially considering what I've been through."

"Mama, you choose the wrong friends to be with."

"Well, just so you know, I haven't touched any drugs in two in a half months and I have a job interview at the doctor's office too. I will be filing, typing, faxing, and sending of letters to patients. I'll be starting next week," she was proud to announce.

"Now that's good news. That's actually the best news I've heard from you so far. I'm happy for you mama."

Monica interrupted in changing the subject, "Mike, you know that son of a bitch Cecil hit our sister. And I just found out that he's been abusing her for a while too."

"Where is that punk?" I asked with anger all in my voice.

"He's locked up again."

"I just wish that Sherita would learn her lesson, because talking to her is like talking to a stained glass window. Well, I'm glad to hear that you're doing alright mama, but I gotta get back to the hotel before Karen wakes up."

After getting off of the phone, I still can't seem to understand why my family has so many issues. Sometimes I believe they bring a lot of perplexity among themselves. I can't allow these problems to ruin my vacation or to disturb me and Karen's life. As I got back to the suite, Karen was awake. I had the flowers wrapped in a golden box with a red ribbon wrapped around it.

"Aawww baby, Thanks!" Karen was surprised. "These are gorgeous. Where were you?"

"I went to the casino downstairs," I replied as I turned towards the closet door.

I felt bad because of what happened with the transsexual. I had cheated on my wife for the first time, *'but I would never do it again'*, I thought to myself.

As Karen walked over to the closet to hang up her robe, "Baby, did you win any money for us at least?"

"Naw, I lost a few bucks at the blackjack table, and then I had a call from Monica and mama. She's out of the drug treatment center and found a job that she starts next week."

He went on to tell her how he also found out that Sherita and Cecil got into a dispute that landed him back in jail from putting his hands on her.

"Honey, that's a lot to deal with. Maybe we should have a family gathering, just you and I and the family so all of these conflicting forces can be put behind us," Karen suggested. "I mean, I know that Sherita and

71

I have a duel between us, but I just want it to cease. I don't know why she's so distance towards me."

"You know why Sherita is like that. She's very envious of what we both have built together as a couple. Let's not talk about this anymore, I'm here to have some fun. I feel like dancing," I ended the conversation about our family issues.

My wife and I decided to go dancing that night and we cut a rug, as the older people would say. We haven't danced in about a year because of our busy schedules. We decided to stay one more day so that Karen could go shopping, which was one of her favorite hobbies. I didn't mind it. I love to see her look beautiful, which was what attracted me to her in the first place. Not only was it her beauty, but she also had pizzazz, intelligence, and is a highly educated woman.

The last day, we just relaxed and made passionate love. I laid Karen on the bed and started kissing her, maneuvering my lips against her soft plump breasts, and when I took a dive into her pussy with my wet tongue, and listened to her as she moaned and groaned. Just the way I loved to hear it. She loved for me to perform oral sex on her. We both trembled until I slid my hard dick inside of her for a minute until she surprised me by getting on top and riding me with such aggression. I loved every minute of it. After our passionate love making, we just relaxed until it was time for us to catch our flight back to Ohio.

CHAPTER TEN

~*A Night Out*~

It was going on six-thirty in the evening when I finally decided to leave work. I would normally get off at five o'clock, but I decided to work an extra hour and a half of overtime. I needed the money and the mail was backed up, which was most of the time due to having a lazy ass supervisor. I had to hurry and get this mail sorted, so I could meet Lavern at this club called *Sho-Nuffs*, located around the corner on Carver Street. She so badly wanted to go out and so did I. I just wanted to see what was going down and to see what everyone kept talking about.

I hadn't been out in a long time. Michelle and Javon had to be picked up from the aftercare program. I had to call to let them know that I was running a little late because of the overtime I had to put in, which wasn't a problem for them. As I signed out for the night and got comfortable in my car, my cell phone rung. It was Lavern, but I had to call her back later since I was driving and didn't have time to hook up my Bluetooth.

When I did get a chance to look at my phone, there was a message from her, "Girl, get your ass over to my house, where are you? I'm trying to get to the club before nine thirty," her message ended. I called her back, but this time I got her voice mail. Now, I'm wondering where her ass was at. I guess we were playing phone tagging now.

After picking up the kids and getting them in the car, Lavern called again. She must have tried to call me while I was leaving her a message. This time I picked up.

"Monica, where are you?"

"I just picked the kids up from aftercare."

"You know it's almost seven thirty, right?"

"Yes Lavern, but we will just have to get there a little late, it's just that simple. I still have to wait for Aaron to pick the kids up and you know how he likes to run late sometimes. So, I need to feed them, take a shower and get dressed. I don't want them being hungry when he comes to pick them up. I have to make sure they're taken care of first. He won't be here until about nine tonight, so if you want, you can go without me."

"Girl, please! Don't be crazy. I'll just have to wait. I really just wanted to catch the two for one drinks. You know I need my Grey Goose and Cranberry, and was trying to see if that Jamaican dude was going to be there too. I think his name is Jay or something like that."

"Lavern, you are so bent on meeting this dude and don't even know his name. Has he even approached you in any way?" I laughed.

"He was staring me down the last time I was there."

"That doesn't mean he's interested in you though. But, let me get off this phone 'cause I'm still driving and I don't wanna get pulled over."

"Alright girl! Well, how about I come to your house and get dressed?"

"Sounds like a plan to me," I agreed.

As I drove up to the house and parked the truck, "Mommy, is Daddy picking us up tonight?" Michelle blurted her question out.

"Yes he is Michelle," I replied quickly as I got them out of the car and into the house so that I could do what I needed to do. Not a minute after stepping into the house, he phone rung. It was Aaron and I hoped he wasn't calling to cancel out from picking up the kids again.

"Hello!" I answered sounding a bit grumpy.

"Hey, it's me. I was just calling to let you know that I'll be there around nine thirty or ten."

"Aaron, you told me nine!"

"I know what the hell I said," he raised his voice a little. "I got caught up in a meeting at my job, alright?"

"Aaron, are you really coming?"

"Of course! I haven't seen my kids in a month. And where were you last weekend anyway? I tried calling and you never answered the phone."

"Oh, I took the kids to Disneyland."

"Well, the next time, let me know first, before you take my kids anywhere."

Monica decided that she'd had enough of the small talk with Aaron. She told him that she had to get the kids fed and had to take a shower before her and Lavern headed out to the club, therefore, she had to go.

"I can't believe it. You at the club? Now that's funny!" He laughed on the other end of the phone.

"Why is it so funny?"

"Because, you ain't the club type, but Lavern's crazy ass on the other hand, is."

I finally was able to get him off of the line and ran the shower, while the kids ate their dinner. I quickly prepared some fried shrimp and chicken tenders for them. As I hopped out of the shower, I still had no idea on what to wear. So I put on a pink rayon jumpsuit with the back out so that it could accent my figure, and threw on a pair of my high heeled white sandals that made me just a bit taller. My hair was already done in flexi- rods and I knew I was looking good for the night. By the time that Aaron arrived, I was just putting on my lip gloss.

"Wow! You look good as shit," he stated as he walked through the door.

"Shit? That's how you feel?"

"Girl, stop taking stuff so personal. I've just never seen you like this before."

"Well...Thank you."

Lavern walked up behind him with her clothes in a JC Penny bag, "Hey Aaron," she spoke.

"Hey Lavern...are y'all ready?" He reverted back to the kids. I'll have the kids back on Sunday afternoon. Are you working tomorrow?" Aaron asked.

"Actually, I'm not. This is my weekend off."

Aaron gathered up the kids and their things and headed out to the car to start their weekend.

"Damn girl, Aaron looking good," Lavern mentioned as the door closed behind her, "he almost made me wanna jump on his ass," she laughed.

"Lavern, can you take your ass in the room and get dressed? Earlier, you were fussing about the time."

Lavern made her way upstairs to the room while I went into the bathroom to finish putting on the rest of my make-up. When she was done, she had on a dazzling black halter top with a pair of tight-fitted jeans and a pair of pointed-toe high heel shoes. She had a figure too, and there wasn't anybody who could tell us that we weren't the shit. We knew we were looking good before we even got to the club.

We stopped at the liquor store to get a bottle of wine and cigarettes for Lavern. While driving, we were listening to that party cut *Set It Off,* by Strafe. As we approached the club, I noticed that the place was packed. It was no wonder she wanted to come here. The men in here were like candy on a stick. Some of them were conceded, but most of them were on the down-low. That's mainly one reason why I can't settle down. I'm scared for one thing. Although I yearned to have someone, most of these men in here had a woman waiting for them somewhere. They liked lying and being deceitful. I did know one damn thing, I wasn't going to put up with that shit, unlike my sister. I just can't see how she deals with Cecil. I pray and hope that she doesn't fall for his bullshit again.

As time went on, the place got packed even more, and it was only eleven thirty by this time. Everybody and their damn mama seemed to have come out tonight. Lavern and I sat at the table until a song we liked came on. The D.J. was playing some real good music.

"Come on girl, let's dance, I didn't come here to just sit around," Lavern said.

"You go ahead girl. I'm actually waiting for somebody to ask me to dance."

Lavern laughed, "You might be waiting all night for that shit to happen."

When the Cha-Cha line dance came on, I got up and went to the dance floor. After that ended, it was followed by *Step in the Name of Love*, by R. Kelly. One girl was trying to show off by doing splits and cross-overs to the song as if she'd never been out before. Once I got finished swerving across the dance floor with this guy, he finally asked me my name.

I told him my name and he responded with letting me know that his name was Eric Devaughn.

"So, are you here with somebody?" Eric whispered in my ear, due to the loud music that played over the place.

"Yes. I came with my friend Lavern, and you?"

"No. I came out alone tonight. I would normally come with some of my Navy buddies, but decided against it tonight. So, are you drinking on anything tonight?"

"Yes, I'm drinking on some Merlot without ice. I like it semi-warm."

"Would you like another?"

I gestured that it would be nice to have another glass and he made his way back over to the bar. As he maneuvered his fine ass across the floor, I wondered what kind of game he was playing or if he was even playing a game. He was much like my type, just an inch taller than I. I didn't really prefer light-skinned men, but he was sexy as hell. He had a sexy body, with just a little belly, but that was alright. I had one too, so I really couldn't complain too much. I was just glad that he didn't have dreads. I haven't dated many guys with dreads other than Aaron, who has them now. However, when we first met, he had a low bush and was much taller than Eric. Aaron, who stood six four with a slim build, could have been a basketball player. I guess that's what attracted me to him at first. These days and times, you can't be too choosey when it comes to men per say. But you don't know what kind of baggage they have tucked away until later on down the line. I'm now ready to be normal again.

Lavern was still on the dance floor, getting her groove on and sweating like a hog. Eric came back to the table with our drinks, along with a red stemmed rose. Reaching his hand out to hand me the rose, "I hope you don't mind," he said with that sexy ass smile that imbedded his face.

"Not at all!" I was blushing. "Thank you so much, Eric."

"You're welcome. So…do you have a significant other?"

Eric was a straight forward man.

"No, I don't at the moment."

"That's a shock to me."

"Why is that?" I asked. "Sometimes it's just not your time and it's a lot you have to be careful about."

"Well, I can agree with that."

"So, are you involved with anyone right now?" I turned the question around.

"No. I was involved with a young lady, but it didn't work. Actually it's been about a month now since we've stopped seeing each other. We were too different," he explained.

I thought to myself, now he's going to dash up out of this club when he hears that I have two kids, but what they hell, "Okay, well I have two children, Michelle who's six and Javon who's four. Do you have any children?"

"As a matter of fact, yes I do. I have one son, Eric Jr., and he's fifteen. He plays football and basketball, an honor roll student, and I'm very proud of him."

As Eric continued with his conversation about his son, Lavern walked back over to the table. I just hoped she doesn't mention any of my personal business while sitting here.

"Hey, girl! I see you finally taking a break from that dance floor," I said before she could get a word in.

"Uh huh. I'm drenching with sweat right now."

I introduced them to one another, "This is my best friend Lavern, and this is Eric."

"Nice to meet you Lavern," he said.

Whispering in my ear, "Monica, he's nice looking."

"I'm going to move on and let you guys continue to talk. I'm going back to the dance floor," Lavern gestured with a wink as she left the table.

"Your friend likes to have fun I see," Eric said. "So Monica, what kind of work do you do, if you don't mind me asking?"

I started telling him how I worked as an Administrative Assistant at the Postal Service and he talked about his work as a Firefighter. Then we went on to describe what we both like to do in our spare time, while continuing to laugh and sip on our drinks, ignoring the music playing on the dance floor as our conversation seemed to be more satisfying.

"Lavern and I normally don't hang out much due to our work schedules. I work one weekend out of each month, with mostly working long hours during the week, until about eleven at night or three in the morning. It depends on how much work I need to finish."

"Same here! Normally, when I have a day or weekend off, I take time to go see my son play in a game. Sounds like your job can be very exhausting."

The DJ started playing '*Just In Case*' by Jaheim, "you wanna dance?" Eric asked.

We walked up on the dance floor and again, he had some moves. I wondered if he could move like that all the time. The next song was '*Wifey*' by Next.

Shit, the DJ was gonna have me sweating soon. He was rockin' this club with his musical flare. A slow song started to play next, and that's when I decided that I wanted to sit this one out, but Eric wouldn't let me. He grabbed my hand and we worked our way back to the dance floor. '*Fire and Desire*' by Teena Marie and Rick James played through the sound system and he held me so tight as if I was trying to run away from him. I felt his manhood start to rise and it felt so good for some reason or another. After the song was over, we sat back down at the table. That last dance was so intense, we just kept staring at each other. There was only ten minutes left, before the club was about to close.

"Well Eric, it was a pleasure meeting you," I said to him with a wide smile upon my face.

"So, will I be able to see you again?" Eric asked with his sexy ass smile.

We exchanged numbers. Not just one number, but all three, work, home, and cell phone numbers.

"Are you going to be okay?" Eric asked.

"Oh yeah, I'm just waiting on Lavern to finish getting her party on. We came here together and I drove my truck, so we'll be good," I was still blushing.

Eric started making his way over to the front door to exit the club, "Okay, well I'll be giving you a call soon then."

After I watched him leave the club, I turned to find Lavern coming off the dance floor as the DJ shouted to everyone, "don't drink and drive and have a good night," over the microphone. We gathered our things and started to head out the front door, when we saw that there was a big altercation outside between these two dudes. Next we heard one of them say, "I'll be back muthafucka!" That was our indication that we had to get the hell out of dodge.

"Okay Lavern, let's go!"

"Wait Monica, I wanna see what happens."

"That means you wanna get left. You know what that means when somebody says they'll be back? That means them niggas coming back with guns and I ain't trying to die out here, so we need to keep it moving. We got into the truck and of course, the next thing we heard were gun shots. I put my truck in reverse and sped off. When we got back to the house I was so tired and so was she, so she ended up spending the night at my house.

Although we both were tired, we still sat up until about six in the morning just talking, which was normally what we did anyway.

Lavern and I were very close since high school and we were able to tell each other our inner most secrets and never heard it from any other source. That's how it was with us.

"You mind if I make some bacon and eggs on toast?" She asked.

At this time, we still hadn't been to sleep.

"Naw, and make me some too."

After we ate our breakfast and got our bellies full, we were out for the count and didn't wake until one o'clock in the afternoon. Lavern had to pick up her kids by six, so that gave us enough time to kick it a little bit more. Again, we just talked and laughed until about four that afternoon.

"So Monica, are you going to call Eric?"

"Yeah, but after he calls me first."

"Girl, you don't have to wait for a man to call you first. You can give him a courtesy call you know?"

"I don't wanna seem desperate. We'll see how it goes. Maybe dating him will be an option for me. I don't want to settle with just anybody right now."

"Well you know I met somebody at the club too? His name is Dennis. He's a chocolate drop and single. He currently lives with his brother and his girlfriend right now. We're going out on Thursday. But I better push off now. It's almost five and my mother loves the boys, but she'll cuss me out if I'm late. But then once I get there, he likes to hold us there until about eight or nine tonight."

"Alright, let me walk you out to the car."

Faces Of Shame

As I got back into the apartment, my message light was blinking on the answering machine and it was Mama Dorothy. What did she want now?

The message on the answering machine said, '*Hey Meme, I'm just calling to say hello and I'm doing fine. I'm working now and already got my first paycheck. I wanted to know if I could bring the grandchildren a gift. I would greatly appreciate it. I Love you and call me back later when you can.*'

She could have told me that in person instead leaving that long ass message. It's no wonder my answering machine didn't cut her ass off. I needed to take a nap. I was still exhausted and my ankles were swollen from all the dancing, and those high heels made it that much worse, so I decided to lie back down. When I got up again, it was seven thirty in the evening. Aaron was bringing the kids home at nine and I still had to wash clothes. I was also supposed to go to the grocery store too. Therefore, I got up and ran to the grocery store to get a few things for the kids. I made it back in time to throw a few clothes in the washer, but I had to finish the other loads on another day when I had some time off. I didn't have time to do much of anything else. Once I got upstairs, I saw that there was yet another message on my machine. I was hoping that it may have been Eric this time. I wasn't even gone that long, but it was Lavern, '*Monica girl, I have something to tell you. Call me back, it's urgent!*'

First it was Mama Dorothy, now Lavern. It had been a very busy weekend. I returned Mama Dorothy's call to let her know that she could bring the stuff for the kids after I got off from work tomorrow.

"Hey Mama. I got your message and you're more than welcomed to drop off the gifts for the kids tomorrow, after I get home from work. Where are you?"

"I'm over at a friends' house. His name is Otis. I've been three months clean and sober now, you know?" Mama Dorothy was looking for confirmation.

"Mama, that's good to hear! But I will see you tomorrow and we can talk about it more then, okay? I have to get ready for the kids to come home."

When I hung up the phone from mama, I hurried and called Lavern back.

"Hey girl, what's this important information you have to tell me?"

"Hey there, are you sitting down? I need for you to brace yourself for this one. I've got some gossip to spread and this is one that you wanna hear."

"Okay, well get on with it. I'm sitting down now."

"Bo, your mother's friend who just died, has a sister named Trina. To make a long story a little short, I ran into Trina at the gas station and she told me that before Bo died, Cecil used to come over there before he went to work every morning. Well, come to find out, Bo and Cecil were sleeping together. Just plain out right fucking each other!"

My mouth and eyes were wide opened, "Trina told you that?"

"She sure did. She said that Cecil was selling him heroin. And let me put another buzz in your ear. Your mother knew about it!"

At this moment, after hearing that my mother had been involved in even knowing all of this, I was devastated.

"She said that Cecil would even spend the nights over sometimes and call Sherita to give her some lame ass excuse on why he wasn't home yet."

"Oh my goodness! I can't believe this. I have to call Sherita right now. She's really not going to have anything to do with Mama Dorothy now. This is very pitiful. That low down faggot."

"Monica, your mother is something else. Don't get mad at me for saying this, but your mother ain't shit! I mean, she slept with your Aunt Vera's husband. Another thing Trina told me was that Bo probably had it all on video, but I doubt it. She said Bo was so pressed for those drugs that he would have oral sex with Cecil..."

Lavern was interrupted, "I have to call you back. I need to call my sister. I'll talk to you later girl."

Before Lavern could even respond to me telling her that I'd call her back, I quickly hung up the phone and dialed Sherita's number. But then I realized that she needed to hear this news in person. She probably wouldn't believe me anyway, but I felt that she needed to know what I just learned. She's so damn head strung over Cecil. I wanted to call Mama

Dorothy back and ask her about these allegations, but I'd see her tomorrow and ask her about the tape, just to see her response.

Just as I started to head out to Sherita's, Aaron was pulling up in the parking lot with the kids. I had no time to head over to her house now and I couldn't take the kids with me. I needed to talk with her in private and Delonte was too damn nosey to be only five years old. I just had to wait until I got off of work to do it.

When the kids came in, they were all excited with all the clothes and toys Aaron brought them.

"I see you went on a shopping spree."

"I love my kids, you know that," Aaron responded.

"Give daddy a kiss, he has to go."

Aaron stopped himself at the door before opening the screen door, "so, how was the club?"

"We had fun. We really had a nice time."

"Did you meet anybody?"

"I don't think that's any of your business," I said as I walked over to help him open the screen door so he could leave.

"Alright, I see you later. Do you work this weekend?"

"You know I do Aaron. There you go asking questions that you already know the answer to."

"Okay, well I'll come and get them Saturday morning. Early Saturday morning!" He reiterated.

When Aaron left, I ran some bath water for the kids. After getting them settled in the tub, I ran some water in my bathtub so that I could soak as well. Then I heard the phone ringing again. I didn't feel like answering it, so I kept right on soaking and enjoying my bath. The ringing of the phone started to become annoying. I can't believe someone would keep ringing my phone like this. As I reached for my bath towel, the phone rung once again. It was Mama Dorothy.

"What's wrong mama?" I thought it was an emergency.

"I saw Lavern and she was talking to me like I was some child or something. She was saying something about Bo and Cecil messing around or something of that nature."

"Yeah she told me that she ran into Trina at the gas station. But please tell me this isn't true mama."

"Yes, I saw Cecil over there several times, but I never knew anything was going on, I swear to God Meme."

"Please stop calling me that. You named me Monica, so call me by my given name," I said in an annoyed voice.

"Baby, please don't tell Shookie. She'll never talk to me."

"There you go again. Stop calling us those ghetto ass names. It sounds stupid."

"Well, please don't mention this to her," Mama Dorothy begged.

"She's never going to talk to you anyway, so what makes you think she will now."

"I have to tell her that Cecil is a no-good faggot and she doesn't need him. And for you to be her mother and allow this to happen! I can't believe you didn't tell me of all people. I have to go to work tomorrow, so I'll talk to you later," pulling the phone away from my ear to hang up, but not before hearing mama's last statement... "Monica, please don't be mad at me."

The next morning, I was rushing to drop the kids off. Michelle rides with me until I drop off Javon at the daycare center. Then I take her to school, which was the next block over from the daycare center. When I arrived at work, it was hectic and a mad house, until a florist arrived with a bouquet of flowers and red roses. I didn't know who they were for. The card read, '*I miss you! I hope to see you soon, Eric*' with a heart below the message.

After receiving my flowers, my day seemed to have flowed pretty well, despite all of the chaos that was going on around me. I wore a smile for the whole day and there was no one that could ruin it for me. I was happy and very prosperous. It made my day!

On the way home after getting off of the beltway, I had to make a stop to pick up the kids before going into the house. I wanted to call Eric to thank him for the flowers since I wasn't able to do it from work, but I called Sherita first. There was no answer on her phone, but then again, she's probably still at work. I needed to wash clothes, so I gathered the clothes bags and headed to the laundry mat down the street. Coming home from being at the laundry mat for about an hour, Sherita finally called me back.

"Hey sis, sorry I missed your call, but Delonte and I went to the movies after I left work. I miss Cecil so much right now."

"And you need to."

Sounding a bit upset, "Why did you say that?"

"Sherita, don't ask me. You know why. Just leave that piece of shit alone. Listen, I'm not going to dance around this shit anymore. I'm on my way over there to talk to you about some things that were told to me and that I think you need to know. So, I'll see you in about ten minutes or so."

"What's it about Monica?" Sherita sounded really concerned now.

"Don't worry about it. I'll see you in a few." I knew that if I told Sherita that it was about Cecil, she'd try to avoid the situation.

I knocked on my neighbor's door, Ms. Hawkins, so she could watch the kids for a bit. I knew that she wouldn't mind doing it for me. I grabbed my keys and my purse and headed out the door. I was driving at least seventy five miles an hour down the street. Once I got there, Delonte was sitting there being nosey as usual.

"Boy, go in the room," I told Delonte.

"Why he can't stay out here?"

"Because I told him to and he doesn't need to be in grown folk business. That's his problem now and you don't do or say nothing about it. Anyway…," interrupting myself out of frustration, "I have something important to talk to you about."

"Ma, can I have some french fries and chicken nuggets?" Delonte asked before heading to the room.

"Go ahead Delonte. Look in the pan on the table and go in the bedroom like your aunt told you to."

"Now, I'm going to start from the beginning and then I will tell you the good news about me later."

I went on to tell her about how Lavern called me yesterday and told me that she saw Trina at the gas station and mentioned that Bo and Cecil were sleeping together and that Mama Dorothy knew about it. I also told her how there may have been a videotape with them on it.

"Yes honey, those nigga's are gay!"

"I don't believe that shit! Lavern's always trying to start some bullshit. I know for a fact that Cecil don't like no man. Not as hard and thuggish as he is." Sherita said out of being in denial.

"So you are saying…"

Sherita interrupted my sentence, "I'm not saying you, but Lavern is saying that Cecil is a homo or better yet, a down low brother?"

"Yes and you need to leave his ass alone. I'll call Lavern and you can talk to her."

I got on the phone to call Lavern so that she could hear the shit straight from the horses' mouth.

"Hey Lavern, it's me, Monica. Hold on a minute, I'm putting you on speaker. I just told Sherita what you told me the other day and she doesn't believe me. Please enlighten her ass."

"Monica is telling you the truth Sherita. You need to let his ass rot in jail." Lavern continued her conversation over the speaker phone and told Sherita the same exact thing that she'd told me earlier. The story didn't change one bit. Sherita just sat there with her mouth wide open and her eyes were filled with tears.

"I told her Lavern, and if she goes back to him, that's it!" The conversation was over and I hung up the phone. There was much of nothing else to say to Sherita other than what was just told to her.

"Have you talked to Nathan lately?"

"No. We are just friends. My heart belongs to Cecil."

"And my foot belongs in your ass! I swear to God, if you go back to him…," Sherita interrupted me yet once again, as she always does.

"Okay sis, if you say so."

"No Sherita, it should be your decision when it comes to you being happy, but I can't excuse this shit with Cecil. He's not making you happy and right now you're not a happy camper and you know it. How can you be so naive to this situation? Cecil is sleeping with a man, not a woman, but a fuckin' man!"

By this time, I was mad because she just wasn't getting the picture. She didn't want to get it.

"I knew something was strange about his ass and to top it off Mama Dorothy knew about it too."

"You know what? Don't say nothing to me about that bitch."

"Either way, she's still our mother."

"I don't care. She knew about it and she didn't say anything."

"Well you didn't want to talk to her."

With a shivering voice from the pain Sherita still held on to about her mother, "That's right, I can't stand her ass! Then on top of that, he had a nerve to give her drugs and the bitch took 'em. She ain't never gonna get off that shit!"

"She shouldn't be the only one that you're mad at. You should be mad with his ass too. He helped with her addiction. Thank God she's getting herself together now."

"Sis, how many times have we heard that same song play out?"

"Well, let's just hope for the best."

Still being the bull headed person that she'd always been, "I'm not hoping for shit, but you can hope for the best if you want."

"Alright Sherita, I have to go now. It's getting late and you have to go to work tomorrow and so do I. I'll see you later."

I left Sherita's apartment and couldn't believe how she was acting, even after hearing it from someone else's mouth. I couldn't concentrate on driving down the road. Just the thought of Cecil and Bo going at it with each other was sickening. When I drove up to my driveway, my cell phone rung and it was Eric.

"Well hello there," I answered.

"Hey stranger," he replied.

"Are you busy? I'm just coming from my sister's house and I just pulled up to the house. Can I call you as soon as I get in?"

"Sure, that's a bet."

I picked the kids up from Ms. Hawkins house. After I get them to bed, I had some peace and quiet to call Eric back.

I thanked him for the roses and flowers that he'd sent earlier that day. We continued to talk on the phone about each other's ages. It was something neither of us mentioned when we met at the club the other night. I found out that he was thirty six years old and he wanted to know if that was too old for me. He told me how much he really liked me.

Although it was a late call, we managed to set a date to have dinner next Friday night. He got off at three thirty, where as I didn't get off until about six and then had to pick up the kids. So we set a date for nine o'clock to meet up. Since Aaron wasn't picking the kids up until the following weekend, I would have to ask my neighbor again if she would keep an eye on them for me.

Friday had finally approached and I couldn't wait to see Eric. The kids were with Ms. Hawkins and I was ready to hit the town. I looked out the window and saw Eric pull up in his detailed, burgundy Lincoln Navigator. I didn't even wait for him to get out of the truck to come up to the door. Instead, I met him as he got out of the truck. He was such a gentleman. He walked to the passenger side and opened the door for me.

On the way to dinner, we were listening to various types of music, which ranged from Jazz and Slow Jams to soothe the mood. We reached our destination at an Italian Restaurant. We walked in and it was amazing. There were dazzling chandeliers almost over every table. The aroma alone would have knocked you off your feet. The waiter that seated us was very polite. I thought to myself, '*I need to get use to this*'. I was normally the one to go out and get a chicken special from the Chinese carry-out and a booty call. When the waiter came back over to the table, and gave us the menu, he asked if we'd like to start off with something to drink.

We placed our drink order for the waiter and I noticed that Eric was staring at my eyes. They were light 'cat-eye' brown. It was always the first thing that men noticed about me, not to mention my fat ass, of course.

The night was going very well and I loved every minute of it. We ordered our food and had great conversation, as always. We laughed and talked a little more as the night went on. After motioning for the waiter, Eric reached in his wallet and slid out his credit card to pay for dinner. It felt so good to not have to pay for anything and I felt like a princess at this point.

We left the restaurant and headed towards the truck when Eric turned me around and gave me a kiss on the cheek. That peck almost made my body tremble. Once we got in the truck, he leaned over and gave me a long passionate kiss. I wanted him so bad at this point, I could really feel it.

"So, are you busy next weekend?" He asked me while still looking me straight in the eyes.

"No!" I replied quickly. '*Hell, I wished it was now*', I spoke under my breath.

"Well, would you like to spend some time with me away from here?" He asked on our way driving back to my house.

"I would love that. Of course!"

As I got out of the truck, I couldn't help but to wonder where he would be taking me. He wouldn't answer me when I asked him earlier. He just told me that it would be a surprise for me. During dinner, I told him how I seldomly had time to get away for myself due to working so much. Eric walked me up to my door and we ended the night with another one of his powerful kisses.

"Good night Eric. Dinner was lovely."

"I'm glad you enjoyed yourself. I'll call you tomorrow?"

"That will be nice. That's if I don't call you first," we laughed.

The next morning as I got out of the bed, I couldn't stop thinking about the night that I just had. Eric had been on my mind while I prepared breakfast for the kids, while taking my shower, on the way taking the kids to school, basically all that morning. I wanted to call Lavern and tell her too, but I decided to let it marinate a bit and tell her later on after work.

"Hey Lavern, are you busy?"

"No. What's up with you girl?"

"I went out with Eric last night!" I was so excited.

"Really? Where did y'all go?"

"He took me out to this nice Italian restaurant for dinner. We were kissing so deep that I almost wanted to give him some pussy right there in his truck."

"What?" She asked while laughing loudly.

"So, have you talked to Dennis at all since you guys met at the club?"

"Oh yeah. We went to the movies earlier today. He's okay, but he's a player. I think I have to get to know Dennis a little bit more though."

"Well, just date then, like you always tell me."

"But Monica, don't place all your eggs in one basket. You know how these men are. They're sweet and kind in the beginning, and then they can be hell on wheels later."

"I know that much. So can women Lavern. I'm willing to see how things go with Eric."

The next week rolled around and I couldn't wait for Aaron to pick the kids up. As they were leaving, I gave the kids a big kiss on the cheek and waited for Eric to come. When he arrived, it was about eleven o'clock that night. I had my overnight bag all packed up. I had underwear, lingerie, toothbrush, and condoms. I had all of the personal things that I needed. We left my house and pulled up in front of his place, a two bedroom townhouse, which was about thirty to forty minutes away. I walked in and notice how clean it was. He had nice blue leather furniture with mostly everything else being dark blue. At least now I knew what his favorite color was.

"I love your home Eric. It seems nice and cozy."

"Thank you! Would you like something to drink? Wine, Brandy or Vodka?"

"Sure. I'll take Vodka and Cranberry, thank you. May I use your bathroom?"

"No problem. It's upstairs to your left."

I really just wanted to see how he kept it. It was black and blue, very becoming. I walked around to take a look at his bedroom and it too was of a Navy Blue. There was also an extra bathroom off to the side, but that room had a rose on the bed with black satin sheets and a dimmed red light. I made my way back downstairs and sipped on my drink that he'd made for me.

"Would you like me to put on some music?"

"Yes, that would be nice." I was still checking out how nicely his place was laid out to be a bachelor. He put on some slow music, reached out his hand for mine and we danced and kissed. After we finished dancing, he sat me down on the couch, stooped in front of me, and pulled up my shirt. Then he slowly massaged my breasts with his hands and then his warm tongue. I knew I didn't wear a bra for a reason. By this time, I was mesmerized. Next thing you know, we both were naked. He then graduated to sliding his already erect dick inside me, while I caressed and kissed him all over his chest. Damn this felt good. It started to get a bit more intense as R. Kelly's '*Twelve Play*' started playing. After a while, he led me upstairs into the bedroom where he laid me down and continued to long stroke me over and over again.

The next morning while I was asleep, I started to feel his tongue between my legs, where he kissed and licked me. It was then that we made love over and over. Afterwards, we got up and went to take a shower, he turned me around and fucked me from behind, fast and hard until we ended back in the bed, where we continued our love making.

"You like it baby?" He asked me.

"Yes baby, I love it!"

I thought to myself, '*I hope to continue loving it.*'

CHAPTER ELEVEN

~Pointing Fingers~

Through my clouded bedroom window, from the rain and dirt they collected from the storm last night, I stared out of the window as drops of tears fell from my eyes. I was terribly upset about the news that Monica told me the other day about Cecil. Because of this bit of information, now I needed to have an HIV test done. Something I should have done anyway, just as a precaution. I knew whatever the results would be, I would still be crushed. I needed to call Nathan, but he was at work and I didn't want to bother him with my drama. Therefore, I decided to wait until he got off tonight. So instead, I decided to call my sister, but I got her answering machine...

'*Hey sis, I really need to talk to you. It's about that tape. Love you and see you soon.*'

If it wasn't for that bitch, Mama Dorothy, I wouldn't be going through this shit right now. I was trying to save my relationship with Cecil long before I knew anything about him and Bo. He wasn't any good anyway. I should have known better than to deal with such a loser, as my brother would call him.

I really wanted to see this tape. It was going to be the only way that I believed this shit even happened between Cecil and Bo. Then I

101

thought for a minute, that I should just go on with my life. I know it's not going to be easy to do. I have been with Cecil for a while now. Even if I tried to let go, he wouldn't let me. I would probably have to get a protection order against him if he didn't let me go, even though he was about to be released in the next two weeks, if the judge granted it.

With all of the charges he has on him right now, I doubt it if they would give him a release date. I would hate to see him spend time in jail, but then again, his ass deserved it. Getting back with Cecil ain't worth it. There was really no progress in our relationship and I don't want to lose my relationship with my sister Monica because we are so close.

When we were younger, we used to play together, laugh, and talk about a lot of personal issues. We are two peas in a pod. We hung out together until she became a couch potato, but we still shared that sisterly bond. I get jealous when she talks to Mama Dorothy, whoever she is. I didn't consider her to be my mother. I couldn't understand how Monica and Mike could still accept the way she's messed up our lives, not to mention, her own stupid ass life. I really didn't care if she messed her life up because she's a grown ass woman. She knew what she was doing, and for her not to tell Monica about Bo and Cecil, I was really done with her now. She doesn't deserve to be called mama. I didn't give a damn if I never saw her again. If I did, I would literally spit in her face. I've never had so much hate towards a person the way I have for her.

I listened as the phone kept ringing. It was a number that I didn't even recognize. It could have been Nathan, so I answered it. Until I saw the tape, I wasn't really able to make a decision on Cecil, although, I was getting closer to that decision by the minute.

When I answered the phone, a recording came on, '*you have a collect call from Cecil from Ohio State Prison. Will you accept?*' I held the phone trembling for a minute, thinking about whether I should or shouldn't take the call. I chose to hang up the phone, but the call came in again. I answered it again and it was the same recording. I really didn't want to, but then realized that I should have let the answering machine pick it up instead. Especially after all of the stress he's put me through. My dumb as ended up accepting the call anyway.

"Why did you hang up?" He asked.

"Because Cecil, I wasn't certain if I wanted to talk to you."

"Why not?" He yelled.

"You have the audacity to ask me why? Let's see…you whipped my ass for going to the club. I just wanted to go out with my friend and you had the nerve to get mad? Did I get mad when you brought your dusty ass in here after coming home at two in the morning?"

"Sherita, I'm sorry. I was mad. I was already upset behind losing my job. It's hard for me to find a job when I'm already in the system, and then you go and call the police on me?"

"First of all Cecil, it's not my fault you lost your job. Who asked you to steal that money? Secondly, you're the one who put yourself in the system by not being a responsible ass person, and last but not least, I called the police because your stupid ass was tripping out over nothing."

"I told you girl, I didn't steal no money. I tripped out because you were being sneaky."

"You need to be thankful that I didn't call my brother on yo' ass!"

"Your brother? That's a joke," he laughed, "Here I am waiting for you to come in the house and you out shaking your ass at some fuckin' club?"

"So tell me Cecil...," now I was about to let it loose, "tell me how many times have you been shaking your ass? Or shall I say getting something pumped in it?"

Cecil was quiet for about a second to grasp the question that was asked. "What the fuck are you talking about Sherita?"

"You heard me right Cecil...," there was a beep on my other line when I was about to explain to him what I heard about him and Bo, and it was Nathan. I had to call him back after I got this shit off of my chest. The next thing you know, the phone call was disconnected. I couldn't wait for Cecil to call me back because I was going to reveal everything to him that I knew. I was ready to let his ass go. After telling me that I asked to be bruised for going out and not coming home? I didn't care at this point if his ass rotted in that jail cell. He should be used to it. He's been in there before. A loser is always going to be a loser.

As I stepped into the shower, the phone rang again. I turned off the shower and answered the call.

"Hello."

"Yeah! I wanna know what the hell that sarcastic ass question was that you asked just a few minutes ago." You could hear the anger in his voice by this time.

"If it's the way you heard it, then it is what it is." I didn't even give him time to respond to that comment, "Listen here. Did you know that Bo died?"

"Who the fuck is Bo?"

"Cecil, don't play dumb with me. You know who I'm talking about."

"Alright. Your mother's friend."

"WHATEVER! Well, I just found out about your down-low dirty ass," I yelled through the phone.

"Who's down-low?"

"MONICA TOLD ME ABOUT YOU AND BO FUCKIN' EACH OTHER CECIL!" I'm sure that by this time, all of my neighbors could hear me.

"Man, your sister is a damn lie," he denied the claim.

"Yeah, we'll see whose lying when Lavern gets the tape from Trina. So is it true Cecil?" I wanted to give him one more chance to come clean with me.

"Nope, and I'll stick to that shit 'til the day I die."

"Well, guess what? You can stick to whatever you want to, but it's over between us, and I'm sticking to that shit until the day that I die. How 'bout that?"

"Oh…It's never over!" Cecil threatened.

"Really Cecil? Oh, I can show you better than I can tell you."

"Okay, and you'll see what'll happen to your skeezin' ass when I get outta this joint. You can go ahead and get a restraining order if you want to. I don't give a fuck! How you just gonna give up on me like this?"

"We're not making any progress anyway. It's going nowhere fast. We don't have a car and stuck living in a one bedroom apartment in a crime ridden neighborhood. I don't want my son to live like this."

"Your son? That's all that matters to you Sherita."

"So what…he's my baby. Look Cecil, just leave me alone and do your own thing." I said before I hung up and went to take my much needed shower.

With all of the stress, I ended up with a headache. When I got out of the shower, I called Monica to let her know about the conversation that I just had with Cecil. I told her how I decided to tell him that our relationship was over and how he turned around and threatened me afterwards. I told her that I was on my way to put out a restraining order on Cecil, once again.

"So, where have you been all weekend?" I asked, since I hadn't heard much from her.

"Well, I went away for the weekend with this guy that I met. His name is Eric and he's a Firefighter." Monica continued giving more details about Eric and how he has a fifteen year old son and how he's so much into sports.

"You go girl. It's about damn time." I told her laughing.

"What are you doing next Saturday?"

"Nothing. Sunday, I'm taking Delonte to Champagnes' son's birthday party. Why? What's going on?"

"I'm going to be giving a dinner party over at my house at eight o'clock and I want you to come over and meet Eric." She said excitedly.

"That sounds good to me. I just hope you're not inviting what's her name and you know who I'm talking about."

"I don't think Mama Dorothy is coming anyway and no, I didn't invite her. But, I'm on my way out to the Plaza to meet Eric. We have to get a few items for the party. I'll see you soon though." Monica said before getting off of the phone.

Later on that night, Nathan decided to come over. I was too upset to have sex, so we just sat up and talked for a while and then he left.

Saturday night came and my Aunt Vera came to pick up Delonte and I so that we could head over to Monica's place for dinner. By the time we got there, Mike and Karen were already there.

"Hey Sherita," they both spoke and then gave me a big hug.

Monica was in the kitchen mixing up some banana pudding, so I headed in that direction to see what else was on the menu. I saw that there was baked chicken, barbeque meatballs, tossed salad, rice, collard greens that Aunt Vera cooked, and dinner rolls. For desert, there was banana pudding and lemon cake.

"Why didn't you invite Nathan?" Monica asked me.

"He had to work overtime. I won't see him until Friday."

"Oh okay. What do y'all have planned? Anything exciting?" She asked with this big ole grin on her face.

"I don't know. We may just go to the movies, bowling, or something."

I headed back into the living room to socialize with everybody. I was glad that Aunt Vera came to the dinner, as well as coming to give us a ride here.

I strolled back into the kitchen to let Monica know that her friend had just arrived and Lavern followed as well, with her friend Dennis.

"Girl, he's nice looking." I said complimenting her latest catch.

"Thank you sis! I'm taking it easy. I just don't want to get hurt."

Everyone who was to arrive did. Eric was introduced to the family and it was time for dinner. We all ate as if it were Thanksgiving Day. There was not one peep from anyone, it was just that good. After we finished eating, we all sat around the table laughing and talking until that no good woman walked in.

"Okay, I've got to go. I'm not staying here if she stays." I made it clear to everyone as I stood up from the dinner table.

"No Sherita, don't go!" Monica stood from the table as well.

"I thought you said that she wasn't bringing her ass over here Monica?" My head was steaming at this point.

"I'm leaving too Monica." Aunt Vera said.

Mama Dorothy didn't feel welcomed as soon as she walked into the house, "Monica I'm going to just leave. I'm sorry."

"YEAH BITCH, LEAVE!!" I yelled from the top of my lungs.

Mama Dorothy turned back around and closed the door back behind her, "Now look Shookie, I'm still your mother whether you like it or not."

"You ain't shit to me and Shookie is not my fuckin' name. I hate you. Yo ass ain't worth a penny to me."

Monica walked up towards me, "and you can just get outta my face Monica," I expressed while tears formed in my eyes.

Mike and Karen walked up to me and held me as I burst into tears, "How can y'all just keep being around her?" I asked.

Mike replied while rubbing my back, "believe me Sherita, I'm hurt how Mama let those drugs destroy her and the family too."

I cleared my tears a bit, "Y'all know what this bitch did? She knew my man and her friend were fuckin'. This bitch is heartless. All she cares about is getting her next fuckin' high.

Monica interrupted, "I know sweetie, but she is still our mother. I know how you feel."

"Why don't you do everyone a favor and just leave?" Aunt Vera stated as she and I started gathering our things from the closet.

"You can't tell me to leave my daughter's house Vera."

"Your daughter?" Aunt Vera turned to face Dorothy, "You don't have the right to call them your daughters or your son."

"Shut your mouth," Dorothy lashed back as Aunt Vera charged towards her.

Mike, Eric, and Dennis had to hold Aunt Vera from whaling on Dorothy. Not to mention she's already had a few drinks in her. I wanted to whip her ass too. As things started to calm down a bit, Monica apologized to everyone for the drama and explained that we had a few family issues. I hope Monica wasn't mad with me.

Mike walked Mama Dorothy out so that she could leave. Monica turned on some music to kill the drama and continue where we last ended. It was getting late. It was already after twelve and I knew it was time for us to get going, so I went upstairs to use the bathroom. As I opened the door to come out, Monica and Eric were standing in the hallway with their lips locked. '*Must be nice*,' I said to myself as I made my way back into the living room area. I was glad that my sister finally found herself a boyfriend.

Aunt Vera dropped me and Delonte off at home. "I'm going to call Monica and tell her I didn't mean to cause a scene, but that woman makes me sick. Dot may be my sister, but I have nothing to say to her. Especially after she took money from me and slept with my husband. I really don't think I can ever forgive Dot for what she did." Aunt Vera finished with her venting.

110

Before getting out of the car, I leaned over and gave her a kiss on the cheek, "See you later Auntie."

The next day I took Delonte over to the birthday party at Champagne's house. There were a lot of kids jumping all over her mother's raggedy ass furniture, but they said nothing about it. I really wasn't in a good mood after last night's fiasco. But I watched my son have a good time and it made me happy to see that he was happy.

The following Friday, Nathan came over and treated us to the movies. After sleeping with him that first night, I really didn't think that he would want to see me anymore, which was the norm for most men. However, I found him to be a different kind of man.

After we got back to the house from the movies, I put Delonte to bed. Went back in the living room with Nathan and sat on the love sofa along with him. We started kissing and feeling on each other, then he unzipped the jeans that I had on. After sliding my jeans down to my knees, he slid my underwear down a bit so that he could finger me. It felt so good. I hoped that Delonte didn't wake up and come in the living room from the sound of my moans.

He just kept fingering me until I couldn't take it anymore. His foreplay made me forget about everything that was bothering me the past few days. He unbuttoned my shirt, and I returned the favor. He kissed my neck, blew in my ear, and sucked on my nipples. This was the best that I'd felt in a long time. He slid me down on the sofa and got on top of me, while administering long and soft kisses, all while removing his pants and

111

boxers. Then I felt his long, thick rod enter inside of me. After a few of his long strokes and passionate touches, I felt like I wanted to explode. As we got more in the grove, there was a loud knock at the door, followed by a yell, "Open the door Sherita!" It's was Cecil.

We both hurried and put our clothes on. I was sure that Delonte was going to wake up now. I started calling the police as he continued to bang on the door like a damn maniac. Next, there were three, four, five, six kicks at the door.

"Stop it Cecil, you're gonna kick in my door," I yelled.

"Let him in," Nathan said as he slid his pants back up from his ankles, "I got something for his ass."

He kicked two more times at the door and it swung open.

"What the fuck is this?" Cecil said loudly as he entered the apartment.

I heard Delonte in the room grunting, but I rushed to the back to lock the bedroom door just in case he got up. Nathan and Cecil had some words and almost got into a fight, until I got between the two of them.

"Get out Cecil. I called the police already."

I was standing there semi naked in front of these two men. My thighs were wet from the sweat of Nathan being in between my legs.

"I ain't going nowhere!" Cecil said shouting. "But I know one thing, I'm getting ready to beat your ass and his."

"If you don't go son, I'm gonna throw you out," Nathan said.

I was afraid that both of them would start fighting in my small as living room. Nathan pushed Cecil so hard that he almost fell. When he tried to regain his balance, he swung at Nathan and missed. I guess he couldn't get a good hit with all the drugs and alcohol he polluted his system with. I needed to put something on before they really got to fighting.

I knew Cecil felt stupid after missing his swing towards Nathan. I went into the room to calm Delonte down because I heard him crying because of all of the commotion that was going on. They got to fighting and I heard my table and lamps tumbling onto the floor. I didn't care if Nathan damn near killed Cecil. I knew I was finished with Cecil. Before I knew it, I looked around and heard sirens going off. One of my neighbors must have heard the commotion and called the police too.

Cecil heard the police coming and dashed towards the door to leave. But because I lived on the third floor, he didn't get far. One of the officers came in to assess the damages to the door, inside of the house, and take a report about what had just transpired. Nathan walked with me with the officer downstairs, where I saw Cecil once again, in handcuffs.

"It ain't over Sherita. Not for you or your little boyfriend," Cecil threatened me again, but this time in front of an officer.

Nathan and I went back upstairs to put Delonte back to bed, since the last officer was coming out of the apartment.

"Baby, I'm going to look for another apartment for you. You need to move away from this neighborhood and that dude is crazy." Nathan suggested.

As he held my hand, "Nathan, I'm so sorry about all of this and for what he did."

"Don't worry, I understand."

Then we were back where we left off, before the asshole showed up and interrupted us earlier. I was hotter than I was before. My mind was at ease again, and I hoped for it to stay that way. Cecil was out and Nathan was definitely in it!

CHAPTER TWELVE
~The Big Move~

The moving van pulled up in front of the house. Karen and I were packed up and ready to settle in when I started thinking about the transsexual that I had sex with. I couldn't stop thinking about what he or she did to me, but I had to let go of this thought in my mind somehow. I couldn't let this happen again.

As we directed the movers to place things where they belonged, I noticed two of them staring at Karen. However, I had my eye on one of them. I tried to ignore them and stop having negative thoughts. I guess they couldn't help it, I mean who could?

She was wearing white tennis shorts that showed off her beautiful legs, and a red shirt that clung to her skin. Her hair was spiraled in tiny curls that hung down her back. I kept trying to look past these idiots, but these guys were really pushing it. Then after a while, I had to speak up.

"Shouldn't you guys be finishing up your job and not staring at my wife?"

One guy replied, "I'm doing my job sir. I'm not looking at your wife man."

"I'm looking right at you!" I said with an eyebrow lifted.

I was bold talking to that guy that way. He was young and with a thuggish mentality. He spoke in slang. His facial expression was not of a person with integrity, nor intelligence. I kept noticing the glare he was giving me while licking his lips. I didn't even have to ask, but I could tell that he smoked marijuana. Then he was giving me this *'I feel like blowing your muthafuckin' head clean off your shoulders for talking to me like that'* look. I wanted to call the moving agency and report this guy and have him removed from the job. I just couldn't bare another look that he was giving Karen, but that would only just show my immaturity about the situation.

As they placed the boxes on the truck, I decided to call Mama Dorothy just to see how she was doing. I hadn't spoken with her since being over Monica's for the dinner party. When I called, someone on her job said she wouldn't be in until later. By the time I got off the phone, the movers were finished. Karen and I watched they're every move, especially with the boxes of crystal, which were very expensive. We brought them shortly after we got married. Although they seemed to be honest movers, you couldn't trust just anybody these days. With all the crime going on in the world, there was no telling what would happen.

"Baby, the men are finished the job. Let's gear up and follow them out," Karen said.

The house was about fifteen minutes away from where we were moving from. Karen jumped in her jag and I followed her in my truck. On the way to the new house, Karen and I pulled over along with the movers and stopped at Subway to grab ourselves some lunch. We didn't want them to be at the house before we got there.

116

After leaving the restaurant and getting on the beltway, I noticed one of the movers raising a Heineken beer to his mouth. I blew my horn to get his attention for them to pull over onto the shoulder of the road. I mentioned to him that I'd preferred he wait until he finished unloading the truck before he started drinking. He agreed with no problem.

"We don't want any of our things broken because you can't wait to get drunk."

"We're professional's man!" The mover exclaimed, "you don't have anything to worry about."

"Listen," I replied, "if you're drinking on the job while you're driving under the influence and drop everything or get into an accident, we can hold you liable? You got that sir?"

"I got it man, but you don't have to talk to me like I'm a child," now sounding a little annoyed.

We finally arrived at our new home. It was more of a modern upgrade Victorian style home with a swimming pool, and a large area where she could plant her roses. Karen loved roses and flowers. It had a state-of-the-art white deck and a two car garage. Inside, there were six immaculate bedrooms with four full bathrooms. The master suite had a separate tub from the shower, and his and her sinks. There was a fully equipped gourmet kitchen with a sun roof top, and two microwaves. The floors were of marble tile, but the rest of the house was carpeted throughout. Karen and I couldn't wait until the movers completed their job, so that we could enjoy our new luxury home. We worked so hard for it.

When they finished, which took them approximately three hours, Karen and I didn't have a lot of clutter. We always were sure to keep a clean home. Too much clutter made a home look a mess.

After they left, we went into our bedroom and made passionate love on the floor. At the same time, I visualized the transsexual giving me that awesome blow job. After we finished, we were too tired to unpack. We didn't want those movers unpacking anything. We were doing it ourselves.

Karen walked towards the staircase and almost fell.

"Baby, are you okay?" I asked.

"I'm just little dizzy and nauseated, that's all."

"What do you mean that's all? Come on, I'm driving you to the hospital." I demanded.

"No sweetheart, we'll be there all day. Besides, you know I have to work on those new schemes that I have to add to the edition that I've been working on for months.

"Was it the sex?" Michael laughed.

"Come on, you know I never get dizzy like that," she replied to his smart comment, "but I haven't seen my period in a month either." she added.

"You mean I could be a father? Let's go to the hospital and find out now," he was all excited.

"I don't think I'm pregnant Michael. It may just be the stress from everything that's going on."

We headed out anyway and I opened the door to the truck and she got in. I usually drove fast, but since Karen was in the car, I took it easy. We arrived at the hospital and went straight to the Ob/Gyn section of the hospital. I was getting very impatient as we waited at least an hour before we were called by the nurse, "Mrs. Karen Simmons…"

I went in with her to find out why she was having dizzy spells. We waited for about another hour for the results to come back, so I decided to go out to the lobby to get a bottle of water and a Twinkie from the vending machine. I loved Twinkies as a child and still do.

Karen was coming out of the ER before I could get back. The doctor sat down to talk with us, "it seems as though Mrs. Simmons is a bit anemic and Mr. Simmons, you are going to be a father," the doctor said.

We were so happy that we just hugged each other from hearing the good news. We both wanted children but our careers were so demanding of us. As much sex we were having, I'm surprised she didn't become pregnant before now.

I asked the doctor how far along was she and he told me that she was only about fourteen weeks pregnant.

After leaving the hospital and arriving back home, I let Karen get some sleep while I unpacked a few things from the boxes.

In the first box, I found our portraits. I put some of them on the wall. Digging deeper into the box, I saw a younger picture of Mama

Dorothy and my father Calvin. I missed him so much. I remember when we used to go the park and play catch, going to the zoo, and the amusement parks. We had a lot of fun until he passed away. I missed Mama Dorothy too, even though she is still with us. I missed that she hadn't had the opportunity to be a better mother. She chose to live on the negative side of life. I know she didn't want to, but she was the one who made that bad choice.

I kept tangling around in the box and found more pictures of Sherita, Monica, myself, and Mama Dorothy. We all looked happy, but those were the good ole days. They were all memories now. I sure wished we could get it back.

When Karen woke up, I fixed her a turkey club sandwich with a glass of iced tea and she enjoyed it. I couldn't wait for the birth of our child. I'm going to be the best father that I could be. I was so excited that I went out to the store to buy a bassinet and a crib.

When I returned home, "what have you done Michael? I'm only three months pregnant," Karen asked.

"I know baby. I'm just too happy about the baby. Let's go out and celebrate the news."

"Where are we going?"

"Let's go to a jazz club and dinner," Michael suggested.

We sung in the car to the smooth grooves as we headed out to celebrate our news and each other. We were as happy as we could be and I only hoped that things would stay this way.

CHAPTER THIRTEEN

~*Surprise Visit*~

The mail orders and shipments were very hectic to sort, and placing mail for the outgoing and incoming mail was starting to give me a headache. It was too much tension in the air. I took a few pills that I had buried in my purse, along with a sip of water from the water fountain. I had to take a fifteen minute break to calm myself down before I ended up having a nervous breakdown.

Since I hadn't heard from Eric in about a week, I was beginning to worry about him. I starting thinking that maybe he didn't want me anymore or maybe he found somebody else. I wanted to call him, but my pride got in the way of that. Laverne was right. Dating was better than just clinging to one person. I should have given myself more than one option to choose from. I'm a very independent and responsible person and I shouldn't have to settle for just anything from a man. The only thing I felt was hurt. He could have least called to see if I was okay. The mere thought of him sleeping with another woman made me feel that much worse.

I haven't known him that long. We were just starting to get to know one another. At least I thought we were. I hope that he wasn't gay or bi-sexual, although that's an understatement nowadays. You don't know who the hell you're being exposed to these days. These damn men just want what they can get from a woman and that was it. Women do it too, but I'm a woman that wants to compromise with my man, understand his needs, and for him to do the same for me. I wanted someone who stood up for himself and have some stability, goals, and ambition. In so many words, I wanted a warrior for a man.

I thought I found that in Eric, but he's gone and I doubt if he was coming back. It was just another ship passing by. Shouldn't surprise me none. It's happened before. I didn't expect this to happen now though. Not with Eric.

I'll be twenty six next month and I began to get nervous about it. I went back inside to finish up my work. The mail was still backed up and it was already five o'clock, which was time for me to go. I thought I would never get off work today. I was so upset that I had to call Lavern. She was the only one that I could talk too when it came to men issues. Then again, she didn't have one, so it wasn't much advice she could give me, except for dating one behind the other.

I got tired of that type of routine. I felt lonely, even when I had a date. Quality time wasn't an option for most of the dudes that I dated. The amount of time spent meant a lot to me. But for them, it was just another booty call.

I thought about Eric all the time. I often thought that maybe he went back to his son's mother. When I got to the daycare center to pick up Javon, I noticed he had bruises on his arm. I was already upset and I was ready to go off.

"What happened to his arm?" I asked the Assistant.

"Javon was throwing crayons and the other child, Bernard, went over to the table and hit him, but he just tapped him," she said.

"With these bruises? Did he hit him with an object or something?" I was yelling by this time.

"No ma'am. I was standing right there near the kitchen equipment," she replied.

"I'm not saying you're fabricating the situation, but he has a red bruise on his arm and it seems as if this child Bernard hit him with something."

"I don't think that Bernard caused the bruise Miss Simmons."

"Well who the hell did?"

"I really don't know, but I saw Mrs. Johnson grab Javon on his arm because he didn't finish coloring his paper," the assistant added.

I headed in the direction where Mrs. Johnson was sitting, "Excuse me, Mrs. Johnson? Did you grab my son and cause the bruise on his arm?"

"No. I didn't grab his arm Miss Simmons," she denied the claim.

"I need to speak to the supervisor. This is unacceptable and will be investigated before I bring my son back in this place." I told her as I began to walk off.

There was a teacher at the daycare center who came out and she stood at least about six foot three. She was tall and skinny. She must have been there for about two weeks because there was another woman in her place not too long ago.

"Yes Miss Simmons, my name is Mrs. Mason. How may I help you?"

I had to look up at her. Come to find out, she was the new Supervisor of the center. I explained the situation to her about the bruise on my child's arm and mentioned that the assistant was seen doing it.

"Well, children normally make up stories and you can't believe everything you hear Ms. Simmons."

"Your assistant told me that she grabbed him in an 'escort' hold and she probably didn't realize she grabbed him forcefully. Now, I'm not the type that gets ghetto fabulous, but I'll just find him another center."

"We wouldn't hurt any of these kids here at Happy Land," she said.

"I'll make out a check right now."

After I gave them the check, I got Javon and left to pick up Michelle from the aftercare program. When I got home, I didn't want to do anything. I knew I had to cook, so I prepared some homemade spaghetti with garlic bread.

After we finished our dinner, I laid down to get some rest, but it was difficult to sleep with all the tension I endured. It didn't make things any better with Eric on my mind, especially since I haven't heard a word from him. Then the assistant put her damn hands on my son. I was so full of anxiety today that I came down with another headache. My throat was starting to hurt. I never felt this much pain in my life. *'What's next?'*, I asked myself.

I hoped Mama Dorothy didn't call me with her bullshit of doing drugs. I didn't need to hear that shit right now. I was stressed out when I had to deal with these episodes. I really needed peace in my life right now, and I wasn't getting any.

Mike called and told me that Karen was pregnant.

"That's good! How far along is she?" I asked him.

"She's three months now," he expressed with excitement.

"I know y'all are happy about that."

We conversed about the move that was made from their old house to the new one. Michael told me about how the movers were acting towards Karen and how it'd made him upset until they found out the good news about Karen's pregnancy. He went on to tell how they needed all of the space that they now have. After letting him express himself and his excitement, he asked how Eric and I were doing. I told him how I hadn't heard from Eric in about a week or so and how I picked up Javon this evening with a bruise on his arm and almost lost it. He suggested that we take them to court, but I didn't think that it was worth it. Besides, I knew of another center right around the corner from me that I could take Javon to and it wouldn't interfere with me picking up Michelle.

Then he started with questions about hearing anything from Sherita. Did I mention earlier that I had yet another headache?

"Have you spoken with your sister?" Michael asked.

"Not since the dinner party at the house, but I will call her later on tonight to see how she's doing."

We continued to talk about Sherita and her plans of finally going on with her life without Cecil. We also finished up the conversation about Bo and Cecil as well.

"Oh yeah, there was one more thing that I needed to tell you. We're planning an all-white party at the Municipal Ballroom next month. Karen has Jacklyn sending out all of the invitations to everybody." Michael mentioned before ending the call.

"Alright Mike, sounds good to me. I'll talk to you soon then."

The next day, before I left work for the evening, I called Aaron to see if he could pick up the kids later on, but he and Brenda were going out to dinner and a movie. It was her birthday. I really had nothing planned, so I just decided to come home and soaked in sorrow. I have to shake Eric off and out of my mind right now. I have to move on with my life. I was alone before him, so why make a fuss about it now?

As I dialed Lavern's number while listening to the news on the radio, I heard that there had been a terrible head on collision on the highway. Why did I come this way of all days? I nominally took the other route, but my mind was far away from my head.

"Hello," Lavern answered.

"Hey Lavern. Hold on girl," putting on my earphones so the police wouldn't pull me over. "okay I'm back."

"What's up girl? That dinner at your house was good and Dennis liked it too." Lavern complimented.

"Thank you girl. How is Dennis doing?"

"He's okay. I talked to him two days ago."

"Well, at least you're talking to him."

"Why did you say that? What's going on with you?"

"It's just that I haven't talked to Eric in about a week and three days to be exact. I called him once but his phone just kept ringing. I called his home number and that kept ringing too."

"What about his job?"

"I didn't go that far. I didn't want to seem desperate or anything. I just feel like something ain't right Lavern. My mind keeps telling me that he has somebody else."

"Like I told you before, men play games. We have to play them even harder."

"But, I'm not into mind games because when you play with fire you tend to get burned. I just think I should move on. This isn't the first time I've been dumped."

"Had y'all made the relationship official?" Lavern asked out of concern for my feelings

"Not really, but I believe if two people lay down, somebody will wake up with feelings. And just so happen, I'm the one that did. I mean, the sex was the bomb and he can kiss his ass off."

"Monica, I'm sure he'll call you. Just be patient. You're probably stressing for nothing."

"I'm not going to wait on it. Well honey, I have to work early tomorrow until six in the evening. I'll give you a call later on tomorrow."

"Okay, well I do hope that you feel better dear," Lavern ended before hanging up the phone.

I didn't feel much like going to work today. I was extremely tired. I talked to my supervisor and told him that I needed to leave at four instead of six. He totally understood my plight. It was around one o'clock and I'd just finished eating my lunch. I finished sorting the rest of the mail and as I turned around, this guy was standing there staring at me, as though he could gobble me up.

"Can you mail this for me sweetheart? How are you today?" The man asked.

"Yes I can. I'm just fine, a bit tired mainly."

"I can see you're fine," he said with a big grin on his face.

I really hope he wasn't flirting with his old ass, coming in here with all that jewelry around his neck and on his fingers and wrist. I was not in the mood.

"Can I ask you a question? Do you have a man?"

'*Oh boy, here we go,*' I thought to myself. "No and I'm not looking for one either!" I answered.

"Every woman needs a man ya know?"

"It's easy to find a man but it has to be the right man."

"If you find a man and he's not to your expectations, you can mold him to your likings sweetheart," he said.

"Yeah? Well, I'm not into molding anyone. They should be already molded. I have two kids to love and nourish already."

"I can dig it. By the way, my name is Percy Mills. It was really nice talking to you."

"Thank you, Mr. Mills. Same here, but I have to get back to work. And by the way, I'm Monica Simmons," I added.

"I know another Simmons very well too. Well Miss Monica, can I take you out to dinner or a movie sometime? Or whatever you prefer?"

I decided to decline on his offer. I had a lot on my plate as it was. Mr. Mills pleaded for this favor and I finally gave in and told him that dinner would be fine. He just wouldn't stop asking. We exchanged numbers and he left. I had to think long and hard about what I just got myself into. The only reason I agreed was because of his complexion. I loved dark skinned men, even though Eric is light skinned. Not that Percy would be my new man or anything. I knew this wouldn't last. He was too old school and a jive talker.

Two weeks later, Percy and I went out for dinner together at this small Soul Food restaurant. This place had a beat up wooden brick front.

It was like a hole in the wall type of place. As quickly as we walked in, I wanted to turn around and walk back out. After we stepped inside of the place, he told me that I could order anything that wasn't over eleven dollars because he had to put gas in his car. I then suddenly loss my appetite after his statement.

"Hey, how about we skip dinner. I'm really not that hungry."

"Oh, don't be that way, I want you to eat," he said while sucking on his bottom lip. "It's just that I don't want you to spend more than you can handle, that's all."

I ordered the chicken dinner with a roll, mac and cheese, and lemonade. He ordered the pig feet dinner with potato salad and okra, a rib dinner, and some home fries, along with two coco-cola sodas.

"You'll have to excuse me. I love this place. Their food is finger licking good."

My eyes were wide opened after hearing his order, "but why do you need two platters? Are you eating here!" I asked because I knew I wasn't staying to eat here.

"Naw, I thought we could get a hotel room, and go there to eat."

Then my mouth dropped, "I don't think so. How can you afford a hotel room when you didn't have enough to pay for the food?"

"That's why I needed the rest of the money, to pay for the hotel room," he said as he took a sip of one of his sodas.

I was glad that I'd drove that night instead of riding in that broken up ass Honda that was in much need of a paint job. I grabbed my chicken dinner platter when the order was ready and headed towards the door.

"Wait a minute," he said. I just wanted to get to know you better, that was all."

"Ok, well you can get to know me, but not in the way that you think. I've gotta go!"

"Hey, you gave me your cell number, but you forgot to give me your home number."

"I work a lot and I'm hardly home. I'll give you a call later Percy," I said as I hoped in my truck.

'*Another Bull-shitter*', was all I could think about Percy. After I took some movies back to the video store I'd picked up earlier, tears started to fall from eyes as I was driving. I wished that Eric would call because I didn't like the approach I got from Percy.

Once I got home, I called Sherita since I hadn't heard from her. We talked for a little while until she started telling me how Cecil was released, came to her house, kicked in the door and caught her and Nathan together. Again, she told me that she was done with Cecil. I'd heard this shit so many times before that it was starting to sound like a broken ass record.

Nathan was helping her to find an apartment, a two bedroom this time, which was good. This meant that both her and Delonte, could have their own rooms. No more sleeping in the living room or bringing company over and not having any private time to herself.

Not only was Nathan taking her around, but he was also teaching her how to drive as well. She said that when she saved up enough money, she was going to buy a used car. She really didn't care what kind of car it was, just as long as it got her from one point to the other.

She asked me about Eric, but I told her I hadn't heard from him and I really didn't feel like talking about the situation. Then, I told her about Javon's ordeal the other day with the daycare center.

My other line started beeping and I told Sherita that I would call her later on. It was no one but Percy. I really didn't want to talk to him right now. I don't even know why I even gave him my number. Desperate, I guess.

"How you doing gorgeous?" was his response when I answered the other line. "I just thought I would give you a holla and see what you were doing on Thursday night."

I rolled my eyes up in the back of my head, "I'm just going to come home and rest," I told him.

"Can I come over so we can get acquainted? Better yet, get to know each other real well?"

"Okay, listen to me Percy. I don't bring strange men to my house unless I get to know them more, not just over the telephone." I was really starting to get annoyed now.

"Why can't we go to your house?" I asked to hear his reason.

He hesitated for just a second, "I'm getting some work done to it and it's a complete mess. But, I promise I'll be a good boy."

"Alright. You can come over for a minute, but just for a minute."

"That's all it would take for me," he said jokingly. "So about what time is good for you?"

"Eight thirty sounds good. The kids will be in bed by then."

I told him how many children I had and we continued to talk, but I ended the conversation pretty quickly with him. He was a bit boring to talk to on the phone. There was really nothing exciting about him. It was just something to do. We ended the talk with him confirming that he'd be over at exactly eight thirty on Thursday and boy was he pressed. He was damn near early.

Thursday was here and it was only twelve after eight. I had just finished putting the kids down for bed when I heard my doorbell ring. I looked out of the peephole and it was Percy. He was standing there with a brown paper bag in his hand. He had no kind of class or style about himself.

I opened the door, but part of me wanted to act as if I weren't even home and not even answer.

"Hey beautiful," he said as he walked into the living room.

My curiosity couldn't be held back, "what's in the bag?" I asked him.

"Oh, it's a forty ounce. I brought this one for you. I thought you may want something to drink."

"No thank you. I don't drink beer."

"Okay, so what do you drink?"

I told him what type of drinks I like to have while walking back and forth from the kitchen to the bathroom, and from the bathroom back into the living room. I just didn't want to be around him really after thinking about it.

"So you drink the good stuff, huh?" He stated sarcastically. "Well, it looks like I'm gonna have to drink this whole forty by myself. You mind if I smoke?"

Okay, so this was like almost the last straw. "Yes I do. You will have to go on the patio with your cigarette."

He headed towards the patio with his pants halfway hanging off his ass. He knew damn well that he was too old for that type of shit. We were sitting on the couch after he came back in from smoking and he did most of the talking. I couldn't get a word in edge wise. I did find that he was forty seven years old. He seemed to make a joke out of just about everything, but he was the only one laughing.

"Don't pay me any mind, I'm a jokester. You'll find that out as time goes on and we get know each other better."

"Percy," I hesitated for a moment, "I don't think that's gonna be possible because I hate to tell you, but I don't normally date men over forty."

"Why is that?" He said surprisingly.

"Because they're out of my league and we don't have anything in common."

He thought about it for a minute and started telling me about how many children he had, thinking that this would make a difference in what we had in common. He had a son and two daughters that he had not seen since they were small. He explained how he'd lost touch with the mothers and hadn't heard from them in years.

It was getting late and it was almost ten o'clock. I had to get myself ready for bed and ready for work in the morning. It was if he had no consideration for what I'd just told him because he wasn't trying to leave my house. He reached over and kissed me on the lips, and then tried to stick his tongue in my mouth. I pushed away from him, but then he tried it again until my doorbell rang.

"Who's that at your door this time of night? You're expecting company?" He asked me.

"Not this time of the night." I got up from the couch and looked out of the peephole and it was Mama Dorothy. This was one night that I was glad to see her. I hope she didn't get back on that stuff because this is what she normally does. It was a consistent pattern of hers.

"I'm sorry Percy, but you're gonna have to excuse me, it's my mother."

I opened the door for her and was sure that she was going to be high, but she had three bags from Sears, one for each of her grandchildren.

"Hey baby, I got off late tonight, but I thought I would stop by to bring the kids their gifts. As Percy stood up to leave, mama's mouth dropped wide open, "oh my god," she said.

"What's wrong mama?" I asked. Looking back at Percy, I introduced them.

"I know who it is!"

Mama Dorothy walked over to the couch, hanging her head down low, to sit on the couch.

"I need to tell you something baby. Have a seat."

I walked over to sit next to her on the couch and she clasped my hand, holding it kind of tight, when she started to explain to me how she'd known Percy.

"You see, Percy and I knew each other back in the day when I was on drugs really heavy and he was one of my suppliers. We actually ran into each other again some years ago, but that was it. We were never a couple or anything like that…"

"Mama, what are you saying?" I interrupted her explanation.

She looked me dead in my eyes, "Let me finish baby. I told you and Shookie that I didn't know who your fathers were and I'm still unsure of whom Shookie's father is, but I can tell you that Percy is your father."

"What?" Percy said while looking puzzled. "Why didn't you tell me when we saw each other last? Oh my goodness, I feel so ashamed."

"I was on a drug mission and I didn't know where to find you," she told him.

I looked at her with such confusion and then stood up to face Percy, "Are you really telling me that this man, who was trying so hard to get into my panties, is my father?" I asked with tears forming in my eyes.

"GET OUT!" I yelled. "The both of y'all can leave now."

"Please Monica, it's not my fault," Mama Dorothy said calmly.

"It is your fault! It's your fault for screwing everything moving and being on drugs," I reminded her of her past.

"I didn't care to contact Percy at that time. I was on the go all the time."

"I think I should leave now," Percy said as he turned towards the door.

"Yes, please leave before I go off. And that goes for you too mama."

"Can I at least leave the gifts for my grandchildren?"

"Do what you wanna do, you been doing it."

"I've missed most of your life and I'm sorry for that Monica," Percy said before heading down the hallway with tiny tear drops in his eyes.

"It's best that you not come back Percy. Have a good night." I closed the door and put the locks on.

The next day I couldn't even get up to go to work. I felt really sick on my stomach. Thinking about what transpired the night before. Thinking about how my father tried to stick his tongue in my mouth to kiss me. I stayed home for three days. I couldn't believe how my mama, of all people, kept a secret from me that long. She will definitely have to give me some time. I'm not in the mood or in the state of mind to see her right now.

Thank God for friends like Laverne. She picked up the kids for me and took them to school. After she returned to my house, I told her the whole story. She was just as confused and humiliated as I was. I took several pills to try and cure my headache. The more I thought about that awful situation, the more pills I wanted to take, but I didn't want to take my life and end up in the hospital over this shit. It wasn't worth it, but I felt depressed and ashamed at the same.

Here it was Mike and Karen was expecting a baby and they were happy about that. Sherita had finally got rid of Cecil and found a new love. But for me, I now felt so violated.

She was nothing but a liar. Mike didn't let her destroy his life, but she destroyed my dignity. Sherita was going to flip when I tell her what happened. Then again, she wouldn't even care. She already hated mama anyway. And now I started to understand why she felt the way she did towards mama all of these years.

Wiping my tears from my eyes, I had to try and learn how to deal with it. I knew that it was going to be difficult, but I had to do what a woman had to do. Mama Dorothy didn't care who she hurt. That was who she was and will always be. She was conniving and selfish.

When I got up Saturday morning, I didn't have anywhere to go. This was the weekend that Aaron didn't have to pick up the kids because I was off. I still hadn't heard from Eric. I hoped that he was okay. All sorts of things were running through my mind. I started to wonder what if he'd died. These negative thoughts made me set aside my pride and contact the Fire Department, and found out that he was not in today nor would he be in the next day. After probing for information on Eric, in which I had to act as if I were a relative of his, I found out that he was on medical leave. When I tried to find out what happened, I was told that they couldn't release that type of information. *'That's why I hadn't heard from him'*, I thought to myself after hanging up the phone.

I called around to four hospitals in Cleveland and there was no information on Eric. I even called Memorial State on Sampson Avenue and that's when I located him.

"Hello, I'm looking for an Eric Devaugn?"

"Yes ma'am, hold on please," the woman on the other end stated.

She came back to the phone and told me what ward he was on and gave me the room number. I didn't even think to ask for his phone number though. Instead, I quickly got dressed and just jumped in my truck and sped off to the hospital. When I arrived, the nurse gave me a visitor pass and I caught the elevator up to Ward five. As I walked towards his room, his son was sitting next to his bedside. Eric had an oxygen mask covering his mouth.

"How is he? I asked his son as I walked in, but Eric was asleep.

"He's fine," he replied.

"My name is Monica," I introduced myself.

He then introduced himself, but I already knew who he was from the pictures that Eric showed me.

"My father was worried about you," he said while holding his dads hand. "He told me about you some time ago," he was smiling.

Him telling me this brought a smile to my face. I can see that Eric was trying to open his eyes and when they did, they lit up when he saw my face. I was so glad to see him too. I walked over and gave him a big hug.

"I'm sorry, but I've been meaning to call you," he whispered in my ear.

He told me that he'd been there for about two weeks after smoke got into his lungs while on the job and his arm was badly burned as well, but he was being released on Monday, which was a good thing.

I felt so much better knowing that he was alright and that it wasn't anything that had to do with another woman.

He told me how he wanted to spend some time together with me and how he needed to make it up to me for worrying about him all this time. I told him not to worry about it and that he needed to get some rest.

"Oh, I've gotten plenty of rest being in here for the past two weeks," he laughed. I wanted to tell Eric about what happen the other night with me, Percy, and mama, but I couldn't bring myself to tell him right now, so I decided to let it rest. Some things are left unsaid and that's the way I left it. I was just glad that I found my man.

CHAPTER FOURTEEN

~*A New Day*~

It was Sunday night and I barely slept, knowing that Eric would be discharged from the hospital in the morning. I guess I experienced sleepless syndrome, since I felt bad for not contacting him sooner than I did. When I finally got up the next morning, I wondered if he had someone that was going to pick him up after his discharge. I knew that I had to work, but instead, I called to let my supervisor know that I would be in a bit later than usual, and he was okay with that. He knew I was a damn good worker so it was his pleasure. Therefore, I called Eric to let him know that I'd be there to pick him up if he didn't already have a plan. He didn't, and I was glad.

I arrived at the hospital the next morning and he was getting packed up to leave.

"How are you?"

"I'm fine," he said before giving me a kiss on the lips.

The nurse arrived with a wheelchair to escort him to the lobby where he received his discharge papers. We then left the hospital and I could see that Eric was staring at me. He was so happy to see me and I was happy to see him as well. I dropped him off at home, got him in the house and made sure that he was comfortable before I left him to head to work for the day.

Later that evening after I got off work, I went over to Sherita's to drop off the gift that Mama Dorothy left for Delonte.

She opened the door with a smile big enough to light up Broad Way. She seemed so happy that I didn't want to tell her what happened the other night. I hadn't seen her so happy in a long time and I really didn't want to spoil her day, but I had to tell her anyway.

"Hey Sis," she invited me into the apartment.

"What's up Sherita?"

"Mama Dorothy left this gift for Delonte."

"I shouldn't take this shit. What is it? He already has one of these. I should break this shit and throw it in her face." It was a hooked on phonics learning game.

"She gave Michelle a Barbie Head doll with a make-up compartment attached to it, and Javon got a hooked on phonics learning game too."

"Her ass is feeling guilty now. That's why she's doing this."

"Well," I interrupted her rage about mama and the gifts. "What I'm about to tell you is going to trip you out, so you need to have a seat."

"Oh my God, what happened now?"

"Let me start from the beginning…" I reiterated to her about me not hearing from Eric for the past couple of weeks and how I'd met this guy named Percy Mills while at work. I told her how we'd met up that

142

same night for dinner and ended back up at my place afterwards. I went into the whole spill about him trying to be so persistent with me, as to kiss me and even try to tongue me down when Mama Dorothy showed up at the door with gifts for the children.

"When mama walked in, she was in complete shock." Sherita was paying full attention as not to miss anything that I was telling her and didn't interrupt me at all.

"Come to find out, this nigga is my father!"

"Oh my goodness. You playin' right?" She asked me.

"Hell no, I ain't playin'."

"That bitch! You see why I can't stand her ass now don't you? She told us she didn't know who neither one of our fathers were."

"I guess she knew that Percy was my father though, but just never said anything."

"Uh huh…so how you feel about it?" Sherita asked as she got up and made her way into the kitchen to fix some coffee.

"I feel humiliated and embarrassed. I've been having funny feelings about this ever since it happened."

"Yeah girl, you should have punched her in the face. That's what the fuck I would have done."

"No Sherita, she's still our mother, regardless of any situation. I'm just upset because she knew all of this time who my father was and never said a word to me! She doesn't know it yet, but it's gonna be a long time before I can trust or talk to her again."

"You already know that I'm not ever going to talk to her ass, so…" Sherita reiterated to me.

"I'm not going to say never, but I just need some time that's all."

"She used drugs half the time. Shit, most of the time she never came home. We always had to stay over Aunt Vera's house because the bitch barely had food for us to eat. Remember when Aunt Vera had to sacrifice to buy us school clothes? We should have called her mama for real. I remember everything that bitch took us through and that's why I hate her ass so bad. Aunt Vera has always been there for us and you know it," Sherita ended her venting.

"I agree with you. Mama did try sometimes though. She went out tricking just to get food for us to eat you know?" Monica told her because Sherita was too young to remember that part.

"I don't care. I remember one occasion when she spent all her money on dope and we had to eat peanut butter on bread with no jelly and Mike had to ask our neighbors for the peanut butter. I know I was young, but I remember everything that bitch did and that was foul. Then she turned around and fucked Uncle Harold behind Aunt Vera's back."

Sherita went on to tell me how she remembered being fifteen and talking to Champagne on the phone one night, being sneaky, and how they were trying to figure out a way to go to the movies. They snuck out and didn't come back until after midnight. She said when she went into the kitchen to eat some ice cream and cookies, she saw that we didn't have any juice left in the fridge, so she went into mama's room to ask her about it.

"The bitch didn't even have sense enough to lock the door. That's when I saw Uncle Harold fucking the bitch. When she saw me, the only thing she could do was yell at me for just coming into her room without knocking. I slammed her fucking door so hard, you should have heard it tremble."

"Did they come out of the room after that?" I asked.

"Nope. Uncle Harold stayed in there for a while longer. He didn't leave until about around two in the morning. From then on, I couldn't stand her ass. It wasn't just that, it was the way she carried herself and called herself being somebody's mother. I felt as though she hasn't been much of a mother to me, you, or Mike."

"Damn Sherita, I didn't know you caught her bed in with Uncle Harold?" Although it had been a long time ago, my jaws were tight from hearing some disgusting shit like that.

"I just think mama needs help and maybe one day she can get it." I interrupted the conversation on mama and switched it to Eric.

"I found out that Eric was in the hospital all this time from being injured on the job while putting out a fire. I picked him up from the hospital this morning. But we're having dinner tonight at the Seafood Palace on Smithfield St., so let me get going so I can get dressed and I'll talk to you later."

After getting in the house, I had a message on my answering machine from Eric, '*Hey sweetie, I would like you to bring Michelle and Javon to dinner as well if that's okay with you. Call me back and let me know. Talk to you soon.*' I called him back asking why he wanted the kids to come along and he just wanted all of us together tonight for dinner.

Getting dressed so that I could head out, my cell phone rings and it was Mama Dorothy. I started not to answer it, but I chose otherwise.

"What is it?" I answered mad as shit.

"Don't be mad at me MeMe," she pleaded.

"I asked you not to call me MeMe. I have nothing to say to you right now and I'm on my out so don't call me, I'll call you," I said to her before ending the call.

The phone rang again and this time, I just let the voicemail pick it up. '*I just wanted to say that I'm sorry for everything. As far as Harold and Vera, he kept pursuing me and when Vera and I got into an argument one night, it just happened between him and I. It was a mistake and I'm still paying for it. Now, as far as Percy is concerned, I never knew where he was. Please call me back later, okay?*'

I just wanted her to understand why everyone had turned their backs on her. The thing with Harold may have been a mistake, but that was her sister, her flesh and blood. She never told Aunt Vera that she was sorry, but she kept telling us how sorry she was about the situation. There was always some sort of excuse on why she never apologized to Aunt Vera about that night. I know my grandma Rose would turn over in her grave if she knew what was going on in this so-called family. She only had two daughters and one lost the fight. They both managed to graduate high school and get married. They both, in my eyes, had the perfect life, but my mother had to be the one to tear down the family foundation that we all built together. Instead, she chose to live a life of despair, and now it was our turn to have a life without her in it.

I continued to get myself together and had Michelle to wear her skirt set with a pair of aqua-blue sandals that matched her outfit. Javon put on his Michael Jordan Jersey, a pair of shorts, and his Nike tennis shoes. I wasn't sure what I wanted to wear so I just put on my red and white strapless sun dress and a pair of red sling backs. It was mid-September and it was incredibly warm out.

It was a quarter to eight when the kids and I left the apartment. When we arrived at Seafood Palace, I didn't notice Eric at first and then I saw that Eric Jr. was holding a bouquet of flowers in his hand. The restaurant was really nice and I was really pleased.

"You look nice tonight," Eric complimented me.

"Thank you sweetie and so do you."

Staring at me with those sexy eyes always sent chills up my spine. Not only that, he was wearing Joop cologne, which was my favorite to smell on him. He had on jeans with a black satin shirt, and a pair of black squared toe shoes and Eric Jr. wore a pair of jeans with his tennis shoes.

We had an 'ALL YOU CAN EAT' night. They had all sorts of seafood selections, and the kids bonded well with Eric Jr. They all headed over to the ice cream machine, which gave Eric and me some time to talk.

"What's the matter Eric?" He was just sitting there staring at me.

"Nothing baby. I'm just admiring you." I covered my eyes with my hands while smiling.

We all ate and ate until we couldn't eat anymore. When the kids came back to the table with their ice cream, I made my way over to get some cake. Getting back to the table with my desert, Eric reached in his pocket and pulled out a gold box and sat it on the table. Inside was a necklace with diamonds embedded in it. My birthday was the following Wednesday and he remembered.

"Thank you Eric, it's gorgeous!" I said to him with the biggest smile on my face showing all of my pearly whites.

"Just like you baby, just like you."

"You are so sweet. I really appreciate this," I said getting up and giving him the wettest kiss I had.

We decided to go over to the bar and get a cocktail while the kids continued to enjoy themselves. He ordered a Hennessey and Coke, while I had my signature drink, Gin and Orange Juice, and we toasted to a wonderful evening.

Although it was nearing midnight, I was really enjoying myself and so were the kids. We all just seemed like the happy family.

"You know, if you and the kids don't have any plans tomorrow, I would love for you all to come out to little Eric's game."

"That sounds fun. Of course, we'll come out there."

As we finally left the restaurant, Eric decided to follow us back to the apartment to make sure we got in safe, but after dropping Eric Jr. off at home first.

Once in the house, I put the kids to sleep in their rooms. They were so full from dinner and the ride home made them much sleepier. I came back down the stairs to spend the rest of my night with my man. We couldn't keep our hands off of each other. Sitting on the floor of the living room, we enjoyed a deep tongue fight. Then an article of clothing started coming off one by one. By this time, it seemed as if it were getting hotter and hotter. I stood to my feet and pulled him by his hand and led him upstairs to the bedroom. I couldn't wait to feel him again. I was very horny and wasn't going to let another minute go by without his tongue touching my most private places. I felt safe with Eric and we continued to make love all night long. It wasn't just sex between us, but we experienced warmth and comfort with each other. This man and I, we had a lot in common.

The next morning, we ended up taking a shower together, put our clothes on and took the kids out to Eric Jr's. game at the park. After being at the game for a couple of hours that day, the kids played with one another, creating their own little games.

We made our way home and dropped the kids over to my Aunt Vera's house. She loved to watch the kids because she had no grandchildren of her own, so she didn't mind at all. Then Eric and I hung out for the remainder of the day.

We took in a movie, bowling, and dinner later on that night. We drove to this area after dinner, which I wasn't familiar with.

"Where are we going Eric?"

"Baby, just chill. You'll see."

We started to approach a big brick and cream sided house with a huge driveway that had a one way entrance and a one way exit. We got out of the truck, walked up to the front door, and pressed the doorbell. The door opened and there was a woman standing on the other side of it.

"Hey ma," Eric spoke.

'*Oh my goodness*', I thought to myself. I had no clue that he was bringing me to meet his mother so soon.

"Ma, I want you to meet Monica," he introduced us as we walked into her beautiful foyer.

"Well hello sweetie, it's nice to finally meet you," his mother replied.

"Hello Ms. Davaugn, nice to meet you too."

"Please…" she motioned us into the living room, "make yourself comfortable."

The house was beautiful. Everything in the living room was in pastel colors, but the kitchen was in all white.

"Would you like some dinner honey?" she asked, not knowing that we just came from having dinner.

"No thank you. Eric and I had dinner already, but thank you anyway."

"Okay, well, I have some homemade sweet potato pie if you'd like some," she offered.

"Sure, I love sweet stuff," I accepted.

"That's good to hear because I also have some chocolate cake and lemon marine pie that I made this afternoon."

"Mama, I'm glad you're here because I have an announcement," Eric gestured while kneeling on one knee.

My eyes got wide as he took my left hand into his. "Monica, I know that I haven't known you that long, but I see a shining star. Ms. Monica Simmons, will you be my wife?"

At first I was so excited, my mouth was still wide opened and my lips felt like they could not form the word that I wanted to say. Then it finally came out…

"YES, YES, YES…I will marry you."

He opened a small white box with a half carat cut diamond ring inside. I'd never felt so happy my entire life. My eyes had tears of joy in them.

"Welcome to the family," Mrs. Devaughn said as she gave me the biggest hug I could ever have.

"Oh Mrs. Devaghn, I will be happy to be a part of your family."

CHAPTER FIFTEEN

~A New Mommy~

O ur names were called for the sonogram results. Karen and I were so overwhelmed about the baby, especially now that she was approaching her seventh month of pregnancy. As Karen laid there on the table, the doctor turned the ultrasound monitor towards us.

"There they are," he stated and then announced, "Mr. and Mrs. Simmons, you're having twins."

Karen rose up from the table to take another good look at the monitor again, "Twins?" she asked in a surprised voice.

"Yes ma'am," he replied.

Karen asked the doctor about the sex of the babies and found that we were going to have one each, a boy and a girl.

Now we were going to have two to love and nourish. I was so excited. I was going to give my children all of what I didn't have and missed out on when I was growing up. There was going to be much guidance, love, stability, and encouragement. We were going to be the best parents our children could ever have.

A few weeks later, I received an e-mail message from Jacklyn stating that she was planning a baby shower for Karen. In October, when the day arrived for the baby shower, it was breezy and a bit chilly. All of

Karen's co-workers were at the house, and of course no men were in attendance except Gabby and myself. We went into the family den to watch the New York Giants play the Dallas Cowboys. Neither one of us smoked, but we had cigars, beer, and watched the game on his sixty inch plasma television. I was happy that Gabby was there so I didn't have to feel singled out, although they were my babies too.

Although I was still happy about my unborn children that were coming in a month and a half, part of me wanted to tell Gabby about what happened in Vegas, but I just couldn't do it. I had to keep that to myself. Therefore, I had to concentrate on my children instead, as well as this game that was on.

Gabby and Janice were so happy for us. They even adopted the twins already as their niece and nephew, since we were such close friends.

One of Janice's friends came in with tight fitting clothes on. Her name was Angela, and I felt that she was up to no good. I remembered her from the dinner party that we had one year. She practically threw herself at Gabby once. I thought they had slept together, the way she was acting towards him.

"Hey man, you see who the wind just blew in?" I brought it to Gabby's attention.

Angela wore a tight fitted jean jumper with gigantic holes along the sides of the legs, a leather red belt wrapped around her small ass waist, and red stiletto shoes. She brought Karen a blanket and bottle set for the babies.

Gabby hunched me on the arm, giving me the code to come outside with him. He needed to tell me something about the home wrecker. We grabbed a couple more Heineken's and headed out the door.

"Yo, what the hell is she doing here?" he asked me.

"Hell, I don't know, this is your house. I guess Jackie invited her."

"You remember that night at the dinner party, right? Well, when we went outside to get the organizer for Janice that night, she followed me out there. She was telling me, not asking, but told me to meet her at her hotel room later on that night and kissed me on the lips. I resisted her because I never knew if or when Jackie was going to step outside."

"Shit, I wouldn't have slept with that. Her fresh ass has been all over Cleveland I heard. Have you ever told Jackie about what happened?"

"Man, are you crazy? I've told her that I didn't want her going with Angela to certain places though. She'd probably try to have her out there doing all sorts of stuff man."

"I'm sure Janice is much stronger than that. You've gotta give her some credit."

"Yeah, I know that. That's why I married her, but I do have something to tell you though," Gabby said looking around to make sure that no one else was listening. "I did sleep with Angela one time before, but that's because she kept pressing me. I let her give me a blow job and that's what started it. But I never did it again though."

All I could do was shake my head at him in shame, as we headed back inside.

The baby shower was finally coming to an end. Karen had received things like bassinets, down to baby clothes. Not to mention, all of the things we'd already purchased. At least with the other decorated room that we had, the extra bassinet would come in handy since now we knew that we were having twins.

It was getting late and Gabby helped me with loading all of the gifts to the car, which took about four trips. Luckily we only lived fifteen minutes away from Gabby and Jackie.

As we finally reached the house, I looked down at my cell phone to see who was calling me.

"Hey mama…"

"Hey Mike, I just called to say hello since I haven't heard from you in a while."

"I know, but I've been really busy lately. I have some good news for you…Karen and I are having twins, a girl and a boy." He said very excitedly.

"CONGRATULATIONS to you. I'll have more grandchildren huh? I'm so glad for you both. Can I speak to Karen for a minute?"

I could tell Karen was too tired or either didn't want to speak to her from the look on her face from hearing my conversation and me handing her the phone.

"Hello Ms. Simmons, how are you? How are the treatments going?" Karen asked.

"I'm better. Five months clean, I can't complain."

"That's good, keep up the progress. I would love to continue to talk to you Ms. Simmons, but I have to get some rest. My best girlfriend just gave me a baby shower today and I'm exhausted."

Karen fell fast asleep once she got into the bed, but I stayed up to watch TV. I kept flicking the channels and ended up tuning into a channel where they were showing the birth of a baby. The baby was being delivered vaginally and I almost fainted. It was amazing to me how a child was delivered. Then I turned on a porno at first and it was a man and a woman, then two men pumping each other. I watched about thirty minutes of it before heading to bed.

The next morning I was too tired to get up for work, but I ended up going in anyway. Karen was now on maternity leave and I watched her for about twenty minutes while she slept, then gave her a kiss and left for my hectic day that was ahead of me.

As the days and weeks went by, I became more and more overjoyed. Karen's belly was expanding more and more each and every day. After I got off work, I stopped by the store and bought more toys. I know they wouldn't be able to play with them right now, but at least they'll have them already.

I called Monica to tell her the good news about the babies we were expecting. When I told her that we found out that we were having twins, she was very happy about it. Not only did I have good news to share with her, but she shared with me that she was now an engaged woman. She told me that Eric had proposed to her at his mother's house and she accepted. Everything seemed to be going well and Mama Dorothy was staying away from the drugs and doing fine with it, so she said. Sherita was doing much better too. I just hoped that her and Mama Dorothy could find a way to bond again.

Karen had dinner prepared for me when I got home.

"Baby, you didn't have to cook. I wanted you to stay in bed and rest."

"I wanted to cook for you Michael," she said.

She made baked chicken breast, a Caesar salad, asparagus, mashed potatoes, and garlic bread.

"It looks and smells good too baby."

We sat down at the table to eat. I was a bit hungry since I hadn't had lunch from all of the excitement of becoming a father of two.

Starting a dinner conversation, "I talked to Monica today and she told me that she's engaged to Eric."

"I know she's happy about that, and I'm happy for her too." Karen commented.

"She sounded happy too, for once."

"So what's in the bag, Michael? More toys?" She asked while laughing.

We finished up with talking about the family members and how it seemed like everything was finally starting to come together for mom and my siblings. After dinner, we decided to watch a movie and fell asleep on it.

The next day, Jackie brought over some baby books on how to breast feed and other magazines on how to take care of a child. Karen was now in her eighth month of pregnancy and she was spreading, but she still managed to stay beautiful. When I came back upstairs from the kitchen from making coffee, she was holding her belly.

"Michael, the pains are becoming unbearable," she mentioned.

It was a good thing that I took time off today. I wanted to stay close to Karen so that I could watch her. Next thing you know, the pains started coming faster and harder. I didn't even have time to call the ambulance, so I grabbed her luggage and walked her out slowly to the car. At the same time, I had to maintain the way I was driving, while making a call to Gabby. I didn't need to get into a car accident with my wife and children in the car.

We arrived at the hospital, Crimson Hospital for Women, which was pretty much an upscale hospital built about four years ago. The nurse came out to the car, got Karen into a wheelchair and wheeled her straight to the labor and delivery room and I was right behind them. I had to end up waiting outside the door while they got her all hooked up to the machines.

Gabby and Jackie were always there when we needed them to be. I saw them walking in as I waited in the hallway outside of Karen's room. I could hear her yelling from the pain, but I still managed to keep myself composed. The nurse came out to get me and told me that it was about that time. I was bought into the labor room and the nurses had me to put on scrubs and gloves. We were in there for about ten hours when the contractions really intensified and she was almost fully dilated. I remained calm during the entire process from listening to their little heartbeats that played over the heart monitor machine. After a couple of hours, our children were finally born on December 20th, 2004, Mya and Michael Jr.

Karen was exhausted and I held our children in one arm each with a smile on my face that reached from one ear to the other.

"They're beautiful," Karen mumbled.

"They sure are," I said, "and nothing can take that away."

CHAPTER SIXTEEN
~ All Together Again!~

My wedding date was set for May 25, 2005. I was the happiest woman ever. I started purchasing and looking in bridal magazines and brochures, making phone calls to get estimates on wedding dresses. I chose Lavern to be my maid of honor. Sherita and a good friend of mine, Stephanie, were my bride maids. Karen was my coordinator and also one of my bride maids.

It was Valentine's Day and Eric sent me the most beautiful bouquet of roses to my job, along with a handful of balloons, a teddy bear, and a card of course. That was my baby. *'He definitely knew how to treat a woman'*, I thought to myself as I gazed at everything that just came in.

Later on that night, I presented him with a beautiful card as well. I also got him his favorite cologne, Joop. I surprised him with a linked men's bracelet which he loved. That night was ours and we enjoyed each other a bit more when we made love like we never did before.

I positioned myself in my favorite position, with him sitting in a chair while I sat on top of him, giving him the sweet fruit that he deserved. He moaned and moaned until I heard those four little words… "I love you Monica. Damn, you got the best pussy baby," he whispered in ecstasy.

We were licking and sucking on each other like trying to catch the ice cream before it melted. I knelt on my knees and gave him a polished knob that was out of this world. I was like an opened buffet that night because he just kept nibbling and sucking on my pussy and I could tell that he loved every taste of it. He slid that nice thick ass dick inside of me, placed his hands underneath my ass, and fucked me for what seemed like hours on end. I never felt like this when I was with Aaron, but Eric gave me the fuck of my life. I'd be a fool not to marry this man.

Time was approaching quickly the next morning and we both left out together to head for work. We still lived in separate homes, since our four bedroom house wouldn't be ready until July. It was only twenty five minutes away from where I lived now, so we decided to wait to move until then, to eliminate any complications of the kids staying in their schools.

When Saturday came, it was extremely cold outside. The ladies and I went to David's bridal for the fitting of our gowns. I had to make sure I picked out an extravagant dress. Everyone was there except for Stephanie, but she called and said she would meet us there.

I tried on three gowns, but ended up choosing a strapless white satin one with genuine pearls on the front with a laced veil. The total, along with their dresses, came to over three thousand dollars.

My colors were Lavender and Silver, so I had Sherita and Karen to try on the halter dresses that were chosen for them to wear.

"I'm sorry y'all, I was held up in traffic," Stephanie explained as she strolled into the store.

"Okay Miss held up ass! Come on and try on this halter gown real quick."

"I was tired from going out to the club last night. You know me Monica, I gets my groove on," Stephanie said while moving from side to side, snapping her fingers to a beat that was in her head.

"Tell me about it. I can hardly walk this morning," I confessed.

Sherita turned away from the mirror, "Yeah, why are you walking like that?"

"Cus...Eric tore that booty up!" Lavern said out loud and we all started laughing.

We were having so much fun. In a way, I wished Mama Dorothy could have been a part of this. Even Sherita and Karen were bonding and laughing with each other. That's what I like to see. It was about time that these two got close.

It wasn't Karen causing the friction. It was my sister Sherita that had a lot of animosity built up inside of her. Not to mention, her having that no good ass Cecil telling her what to do. I am so glad she got away from that bastard.

"Although mama couldn't be with us today, I still need to pick out a dress for her. I would like for her to be in a silver dress," I suggested to the ladies.

"Why don't you pick out a black one for her ass?" Sherita said.

"Don't start Sherita!"

With her arms folded and her lip poked out acting like a baby, "Why does she have to be at the wedding anyway?"

"Because, whether you like it or not, she's our mother. So straighten up your face," I told her as I pulled her by the arm to the side of the store because people were staring and listening to our conversation.

"Don't ruin this day by thinking about mama. I know that you're still and probably will always be mad at her, but this is our day to have some fun together."

"Okay, I'm good sis. It's just that every time I think about it, I just get frustrated about what she did to you."

"I know. I'm still mad too. And to think, I could have ended up sleeping with that man. But it's nothing we can do about the past now. The only thing we can do is look forward towards the future. I don't even consider him to be my father. He was never around anyways."

"Have you told Eric about that night yet?"

"No, I didn't tell him yet. I actually don't think I'm going to mention it either. Don't even want to think about that night anymore. Come on, let's go back inside so they won't think that we ran off," I said while we both wiped tears that flowed from our eyes and hugged before returning back to the bridal floor and purchased the gowns.

The ceremony was being held at Mt. Zion Baptist Church and Jacklyn was handling the flower arrangements. The church was very huge and we wanted to make sure that everyone was accommodated. My aunt was doing majority of the cooking for the reception, but we had a caterer to prepare the shrimp and lobster platters, as well as the veggie trays. The music was going to be played by 'D.J. Smooth Z', a very good friend of Karen and Mike's. Although we had the food menu prepared, we still didn't have a reception hall location as of yet.

Most of the places that Karen called were asking for at least twenty five hundred, which was a bit steep, but that included the catering. However, I didn't want to let my aunt down because this was something that she wanted to do for our wedding.

I didn't stress about it because Karen was handling that part of it and I was sure that she'd find a place before time. I mean, it was only February!

I had only three payments left on Eric's wedding band. It was twenty one hundred and I've already gotten it down to eight hundred. I planned to have it paid for in April, so again, I wasn't worried.

Lavern decided to give me a surprise bridal shower and had a male dancer there. They planned it very well because I had no clue with what was going on. When I got off of work that day, I had on my uniform and when I stepped in the door, Lavern had a video camera right in my face, while holding an outfit she'd brought for me.

It was at her house so I opted to change over there. I didn't even have time to rest myself. We got to her house and I put on the jumpsuit. Everyone was there, Sherita, Karen, Stephanie, and some of our other friends. I knew that Lavern was up to something else, but I didn't know what it was. She kept acting strange, even before we went for the fitting

165

the other day. After coming out of the room with my jumpsuit on, I was led to the living room where everyone sat and was seated in a chair in the middle of the floor. And there he was, *EXOTIC*, the male stripper who made his way into the room from the kitchen area. He was black, bald, and buffed.

"Oh my damn, he's got a work of art in that G-string," Lavern said.

"My goodness, I have virgin ears ya know," Karen commented.

"Yeah right Karen. You know Mike gets his groove on too." Lavern said.

"You're right about that, let's party," Karen said all excited thinking about the last comment.

I was having a beautiful time and nothing or no one was going to change it. As *EXOTIC* worked his way around the room to all of the girls, doing his thing, he started making his way over in my direction, and everyone started screaming, "She's the bride…you got the right one."

He came over and picked my ass up in the air and had his head between my legs, which rested on his shoulders. I held on to his bald head and was having the time of my life.

After about a half hour or so, the dancer part of the party was coming to a close. I had received so many nice gifts from lingerie to bedroom toys and lubricants. I was so thankful to all of them for the wonderful party they gave me. I couldn't wait until my future husband saw me in the lingerie I'd gotten.

I got home from the party and had to carry four big bags in with me. Later on that night, Eric came over with some movies and popcorn, which I thought was so romantic. I hid all the gifts that I got from shower because I didn't want him to see them just yet. He knew about the shower and I told him about the male dancer that Lavern had hired. I only told him about the dancer to see his reaction towards it and he didn't seem to be on edge with it at all, like most men would have been. Instead, he just laughed it off.

We didn't have sex that night because we were both too tired.

"Baby, my bachelor party is in two weeks," he reminded me.

"That's good." At first, I got a little tensed, knowing that some girl was going to be shaking her ass all in front of my man. But I couldn't let him see the few frown lines forming in my forehead. Then again, I couldn't really say anything, especially with having the kind of party I just came from.

"Eric, I forgot to ask who your best man was?"

"My best man is going to be my friend Kevin. We grew up together. I also asked your brother Mike, my brother Everett, and my son to be my grooms-men."

"Ok, that's good because I have three bride maids."

"Oh yeah, I invited Sherita's friend Nathan to the party too."

We talked about the wedding only for a little while and then continued our night with watching the movies that he'd bought over, until we ended up falling asleep in each other's arms.

The following week, we all had to meet up at the church for our first rehearsal that started promptly at eight thirty. Everyone, however, was asked to arrive no later than eight that night to discuss all of the plans before rehearsal. Karen pretty much had everything on point with the church, the D.J., and the reception hall, since she was our Coordinator.

The girls all had their dresses and Aunt Vera confirmed with us with everything that she was preparing for the reception. The food that was on the menu was almost as if we were going to have Thanksgiving, in addition to the lobster and shrimp platters that Karen ordered.

We sat around for a little while, talking and laughing, after the rehearsal was over. Then we all headed over to Mike and Karen's for a few drinks.

The next day, I had to pick up Michelle's dress. She was going to be our flower girl and Javon and Delonte both were the ring bearers. While I was out, I went to pick up and make the last payment on Eric's wedding band. My plan was to have it in April, but I was too excited about it, so I decided to just get that part out of the way.

I hated to hold grudges, especially against my own mother. So, since I hadn't seen nor spoken with her since our last encounter with my so called father, my last stop was to go by Mama Dorothy's apartment and tell her about the wedding.

While driving home from having a full day of dealing with wedding plans and such, I constantly thought about telling Eric about the lies that Mama Dorothy had told. When I pulled into the parking lot of the four-unit building where mama lived, she was sitting on the porch reading a magazine.

"Hey baby," she said as I was getting out of the car. She almost broke her leg running down the stairs, she was so happy to see me. She gave me such a big hug.

"Hi mama," I hugged her back just as tight. Although I was still a little salty about everything that transpired, I'd learned not to hold grudges. "I know it's been a minute, but I came by to tell you about this wonderful man that I'd met and that we're getting married in a couple of months."

Tears filled her eyes, as did mine.

"I'm sorry Monica. I'm crying because I'm so happy for you and I would love to be there, if you'd allow me to be."

"You would need a white knee length dress, which I've already gotten for you."

They continued to talk about the wedding plans and what was expected of her at the next rehearsal, which was set for the following month.

"How's Shookie, I mean…how's Sherita doing?"

Her correcting herself with Sherita's name put a smile on my face, "She's fine mama. She's not with Cecil anymore. She's with Nathan and he's wonderful. They've been spending a lot of time with each other and I'm very happy for her."

"Well, I'm glad that she's not with Cecil anymore. He wasn't good for her," Dorothy confirmed.

"I'm not going to grill you mama, but you know that you should have told Sherita about Bo and Cecil. That just wasn't right! But I'm not going to hold you because I have to get going. I have to work tomorrow and I've already had a long day."

She really didn't have anything to say about what I said. She knew she was wrong and she was ashamed by it. I left her with that thought, hoping that she and Sherita could finally make amends. That was something that I was going to have to pray for and hard.

Eric and I were going to take the first down payment for our new home after we left work. Sitting in his car waiting on me to arrive at home, I apologized to him for being almost twenty minutes late due to traffic situations, and from having to pick up the kids from aftercare.

"Baby, you don't have to apologize or explain," he said. "As long as my step-children are alright…"

I loved the sound of him saying that. I was so glad that Lavern and I went to the club that night. I probably wouldn't have known what the true meaning of love felt like if I hadn't met him. I was finally happy. I only hoped that he remained this loving and caring. The saying was '*men change after a while in the relationship*', but right now, that wasn't our case.

We later pulled up in front of what was going to be our five year old, single family home. It was in a nice up kept neighborhood. We stepped inside and there were hardwood floors, a wooden spiral staircase, four bedrooms, and two and half baths. And the basement was fully finished. I was really anxious to see how the master bedroom looked, and it was remarkably gorgeous which had a full bathroom, half deck, and included a fireplace.

Tapping Eric on the shoulders, "baby, I didn't know there was a fireplace in here."

Laughing, "I knew it, but I wanted you to be surprised when we came to see it."

Making our way down to the basement, "Yeah sweetie," he said, "game time! We've gotta get a big screen television in here."

"Oh, I'm sure," I smiled and then commented. "I already know that when it comes to having sex during game night, I could forget it."

"I won't deprive you of sex, trust that."

We weren't moving until the first of July, which gave us enough time to come back from our honeymoon before moving.

I called Sherita to see if she could watch the kids while Eric and I spent some time together. At first, I didn't want to bother her with watching the kids because I knew that she and Nathan had just moved into a brand new two bedroom condo.

I called her on the phone and she answered the phone sounding groggy. After asking her about keeping the kids, she agreed with no problem. I packed them up some clothes for the next day and headed over to drop them off.

Eric and I got back to my place and I had something special for him. I'd laid out a bowl of fruit so I could feed him from it. Before feeding him, I wanted to do something different. I wanted to feed him in the nude, with only the light that glared from the burning candles I had in place. I removed his clothing slowly and then removed my own as well. I took one piece of fruit at a time and fed it to him with my fingers, then with my mouth. I could tell that it was turning him on. His eyes told it all.

After dipping the strawberries into the chocolate and feeding him about two or three of them, he decided that he had enough. I was interrupted by him sliding me underneath him and landing in between my already warm thighs. There was much foreplay going on and I loved every minute of it. My middle pulsated from every touch he gave, until he slid his thick penis inside of my wet walls. I wanted to explode from the inside out, but I enjoying him too much to do so. Our sex was outstanding and we made love until we were exhausted and finally fell asleep.

The next morning I got up and fixed us some grits for breakfast, along with turkey bacon, scrambled eggs with cheese, and toast with grapes on the side. When he woke up from smelling the breakfast that was made, he had a smile on his face. He was so handsome, with a dimple that pierced the right side of his face.

"That smells good baby," he said as I brought his breakfast to him in bed.

I sat next to him and we ate breakfast in bed together, "I'm glad you like it," I said as he ate every drop off of his plate.

I called Sherita to let her know that I was coming to pick up the kids. She told me that it wasn't any rush and that she and Nathan were taking them to McDonald's and let them hang out for a little bit. Therefore, that gave Eric and I more time to do some packing at my apartment before going to his house to do the same.

We couldn't keep our hands off each other and after we got to his house, we got in a quickie. It was about nine thirty when we finished packing and I headed over to pick up the kids. They were tired from their outing earlier, which was good because I was tired too.

That Sunday, I went with Karen to buy the wedding decorations. While we were out, the guys were getting fitted for their tuxedos. Eric was going to wear a white tux, with a lavender vest and bow tie.

His guys will be in white as well, but with a different style of suit. Everything was coming together. The last thing to do on the list, were to find shoes for all of my girls, which wasn't going to be done until the following week.

It was the end of April and our big day was approaching fast. Mike and Karen's twins were being baptized at the church where we were having the wedding ceremony and it started at four o'clock, and our rehearsal started two hours afterwards. That worked out great because everyone in the wedding party was already there, except for Stephanie and Kevin.

"You know Stephanie and Kevin are together right?" Lavern whispered in my ear.

"You're such a gossiper," I told her. "Doesn't Kevin have a girlfriend though?"

"Stephanie told me that they're not getting along and he wants to get out of the relationship. You know Stephanie is a cold blooded tramp?" Lavern said with her lips twisted to the side of her face.

Right after the statement, Stephanie and Kevin walked into the church together.

I asked Stephanie for myself where she was and she told me that she'd tell me later. I couldn't wait until later, so I motioned to her to come with me outside and of course, Lavern followed suit.

"Okay. Y'all can't say a word, but we fucked all night. Oh my goodness, that man can screw," she told us.

Shaking my head as we headed back into the church, I thought, *'what's up with this woman?'*

Stephanie went into the whole spill about how Kevin told her that his girlfriend was a pot head, had recently lost her job, and how he found out she'd been sleeping around on him.

"He can be just telling you that Stephanie," Lavern said.

She continued to tell them how one day, he was leaving the fire station and saw her getting out of this thug's car, and how he found all kinds of phone numbers in her dresser drawer. Said he decided to call one of the guys one night when she wasn't home and he told Kevin that he was hitting it from the back and the front, anyway she wanted it.

"That's a shame. Let's get started on the rehearsal," I said as I didn't even want to hear any more of that mess.

During the rehearsal, I noticed how Stephanie and Kevin kept glancing at one another. I figured that it was their business. I had the love of my life already, so I wasn't going to worry myself or include myself with them and their drama.

Rehearsal went very well. Everything was done right and we really didn't have to change anything. We were at rehearsal for about an hour or so this time. After the rehearsal, we all went to the restaurant to celebrate. We ended up at an expensive restaurant that Karen chose. One plate was between thirty five to fifty dollars.

Sherita looked over at me and whispered, "Why did she pick this place? I can't afford this shit, even though Nathan is paying for it!"

I suggested that we just enjoy the rest of the evening and for her not to worry about anything. We all sat, ate, laughed, and just talked. We talked about everything just about, from our ups to our downs. Dinner was over and we all were getting ready to head home for the night. As we were heading to our cars, I noticed that Cecil was sitting across the street, puffing on a cigarette. He looked disgusting and dirty. He looked like he'd lost weight and hadn't shaved in months.

I poked Sherita to get her attention and she looked in his direction. He then noticed her, "You tramp bitch! I should come across the street and whip you and your man's ass."

As he got closer, it was clear that he had been smoking crack.

"Leave me alone." Sherita said calmly.

"Oh, I have left you alone," he said.

"Cecil you look horrible and you're smoking crack."

"Yeah. So what? You and your phony ass family drove me to it," Cecil said getting closer with every small step that he took.

"Nobody drove you to do shit!"

"Shut up bitch!"

Nathan's face began to frown from the last remark made towards his girl…"What did he say?" he asked for confirmation.

"Who's this punk?" Eric asked.

"It's Sherita's ex-boyfriend," I answered.

Eric stepped and grabbed Cecil by the collar of his shirt and Nathan tried to hit him, but Mike got between them first.

"He's not worth it," I told them.

Mike pushed Cecil back a bit, "Do us all a favor man and leave."

"Go to fuckin' hell son! Witcho fake ass, wanna be, phony talking ass muthafucka…" Cecil cursed.

The police showed up and asked what the problem was. After learning that Cecil had a warrant out for his arrest, they searched his pockets and found a switch blade, along with other paraphernalia. What a way to end the night, huh?

Finally, our wedding day had arrived. Everyone looked nice in their ensembles. My dress was perfect, and all of the men were just handsome. The ceremony started on time and everything flowed smoothly. I was so nervous, as if it were my first time getting married, but the butterflies went away after seeing Eric, my night and shining armor, standing and waiting for me at the pew. I was so lucky to have this man in my life and felt blessed.

The wedding was over after about an hour, and we headed straight to the reception hall. It too was beautifully decorated and very spacious. We had a lot of people in attendance. Everyone had been announced as they walked through the door to sit at the wedding table, but when they announced, '*Mr. and Mrs. Eric Devaughn*', my heart just skipped a beat.

Everyone was being served and they were eating good. Once Eric and I were done with our meal, we went around the room conversing with our guests as husband and wife.

Our first dance was to *Marry Me* by R. Kelly and then to MaryJ. Blige's *You Are My Everything*. Even Mama Dorothy was beautiful in her dress that I picked out for her. I'm so glad that she was able to make it without having any type of excuse. She was always full of them when we were coming up.

We ate and had a good time afterwards. Eric and I had to dash out to be able to catch our plane to the Carnival Cruise that we were taking for

177

our honeymoon. We didn't really have the time to change our attire, but that was fine with me. Before we left, the D.J. announced that we were heading out and everyone had rice and confetti to throw as we were leaving. It was so wonderful!

When we reached the airport, Eric picked me up and carried me onto the plane. We didn't arrive at the ship until a little before eleven that night, which was fine because we still had some time before we shipped off. We were both a bit tired, but so excited at the same time. However, that didn't stop us from starting the honeymoon. There were candle lights in the room, since we did manage to get the honeymoon suite, which overlooked the ocean. We made passionate love until we sweated up the sheets, and loved it. He was mine and all mine.

Later on, we took advantage of the swimming pool on the deck of the boat and we were alone. I guess everyone else were asleep or doing other things. Trying to keep our hands off of one another was a challenge. It was almost like we were in high school or something.

The next morning, we stayed in bed and slept, until I decided that I wanted to do some shopping on the pier. It was beautiful outside and the clouds were nice and clear, as well as the water. We ended up going dancing later on that night, but once we got back to the room, we made love over and over again.

There were two days left on our trip to the Bahamas and then we were heading back to Ohio. I enjoyed our honeymoon so much, I didn't want to come back home. I wished that we had more time to kill.

On the trip back, we finally got some rest. We still had another two days to chill with one another before returning back to work. It was just too good to be true.

The next day, I got a phone call from Sherita with some terrible news.

"Hey sis. Are you busy? I know you just came back from your honeymoon, but I have something to tell you…"

"What is it? Is mama okay?"

"No. She's alright, but Cecil was shot for owing somebody drug money."

"I sat up in my bed and went into another room. I didn't want to wake Eric with my talking. "How bad is it?" I tried to whisper.

"He's in critical condition right now," she said with a bit of tremble in her voice. She was glad not to be with Cecil, but she still carried love in her heart for him. "Champagne called and told me and then some dudes from the old neighborhood told me too."

I went back in the room and woke Eric up with the bad news. Cecil was no good, but I did hope that he was going to be alright. I wasn't the type to wish back luck on anyone, no matter what the circumstances were.

We got up and dressed, and then drove over to Sherita and Nathan's house. Once we arrived, Sherita got a call from Cecil's brother. She wasn't saying much of anything and was holding the phone. Then she broke out in tears as she hung the phone up. Cecil had been pronounced dead about an hour ago. He'd suffered a gunshot wound to the chest and abdomen. I was sorry to hear the news like that, but he was living his life on the edge and those were the consequences of it. He lived a very dangerous life.

Cecil's funeral was that very next week and even Mama Dorothy attended to show her support not only to Cecil, but to Sherita as well. They were finally getting along…talking, laughing, and even hugging from time to time. It's amazing how weddings can bring people together, despite all of the negativity that lingered in our family.

After the funeral, we decided to have a huge cookout at the house. Everyone was dancing, and having a good time, as we used to. We were finally a family again. We came together like we should have done a long time ago, and nothing was ever going to change that!

Although there were still some skeleton bones left in our closets, some things were just left unsaid.

Sherita, Mama Dorothy, and Aunt Vera were all back on speaking terms. Mama Dorothy had been clean of drugs for almost a year now. Michael and Karen were enjoying their lives with the twins, who were growing up very fast it seemed, and he'd never mentioned to Karen about his rendezvous with the trans-sexual a year ago.

As for me and my father, well let's just say that I've never even heard or seen him again. He's never come back to the job where I worked. I guess he found another Post Office to go to in the afternoons. Eric and I, well we were happy with our lives, as well as with the extended family that we've created. The children all got along with each other and it was just beautiful!

THE END!!

OR SO IT SEEMS...

Tonya Phillips

ORDERING INFORMATION

To order extra copies of *Faces of Shame*, please visit us at
www.obpublishing.com

Opal Book Publishing
"Treating Your Work Like A Precious Jewel"

4613 DALLAS PLACE, SUITE 103
TEMPLE HILLS, MARYLAND 20748

obpublishing.info@gmail.com
obpublishing@yahoo.com